The Wedding Waltz Widow

Charlene Torkelson

ISBN:0615476082
ISBN-13:9780615476087

This book is dedicated to all the dancers I have met, all the dancers I have danced with, and all those I have taught. In some form or another you are a part of this book. A piece of you is in each and every character and in each dance performed. You are a special group of people with unique talents. You have and always will be a part of my life. Since the first year I began ballroom dancing, I have worn a small gold band on my little finger signifying my dedication and connection to all the dancers in the world. This book is for all of you who have played such a significant role in my life. Thank you.

Introduction:

The air was electric with crowds of soon-to-be brides, their mothers, and possible bridesmaids scampering around the convention center. The booths reflected all the necessary ingredients for a successful wedding – gowns, cakes, flowers, photographers, event planners, dance instruction, caterers and music. Each vendor carefully displayed their wares with colorful brochures, banners, and displays of their products. The giggling women slid business cards and literature into their carry bags for future use. Some lucky vendors even had appointments made for upcoming visits.

At the booth for the local dance studio, the smiling woman behind the table was dressed cheerfully in a fitted yellow suit with a matching wide brimmed hat. She smiled broadly with a painted on red smile showing lots of white teeth at each question posed by perspective clients. When? Where? How long? All were vital in determining the proper needs of the future bride and her wedding party. After all, they wanted to look and feel good on their very important day.

Groups meandered around the hallways waiting for the big event of the day – the fashion show. This gala was annually produced by one of the large exclusive shops in the city ready to display the latest in wedding attire. The gowns would be spectacular as would the dresses for the bridesmaids and the mother of the bride. Soon the doors would open for the crowds to rush in and claim their seats hopefully as close to the stage as possible to get the best views of the dresses. Little did they know they would be in attendance of not only a fabulous fashion show, but witnesses to a homicide that would leave one woman a widow rather than a bride.

I.

The church in the downtown area of Minneapolis was traditional and historic. It had been refurbished to its original style with sturdy angular stonework on the outside, classic stained glass windows depicting scenes from Christ's life, and the elegant towering steeple with an old fashioned bell hung in the belfry. Inside was inspiring if not a bit stale from the aroma lifting off the original wooden pews and alter still in service in the sanctuary. The magnificent cross was hanging as if suspended in mid air central to the tiered front of the worship area.

Today was a special day for the downtown dance studio. Today there would be a wedding. Not just any wedding but the wedding of the owner of the studio Edward Garrett. Edward Garrett was an established businessman who had single handedly reintroduced the world of ballroom dancing to the socialites of this metropolitan area after years of avoidance. There had once been a dance community in Minneapolis during the 1950's – and a large and thriving dance community at that. Another historic brick building along the main street had been the hub of anyone who was anything in this community during that time. The building had been teeming with dancers clambering to learn the latest dance crazes. In fact the four stories of that building had been a buzz of activity for many years until the day the police had

2

carted the owner of the building away with charges of fraud and numerous other felonies eventually sending him to jail. The scandal of the whole mess had tarnished the name of ballroom dancing in the city for several years until Edward Garrett arrived in the late 1960's to revitalize the industry with a new sense of morality and upstanding citizenship that slowly brought back the wealthy of the community to the skills and pleasures of dancing.

People – the beautiful people – couldn't wait to learn the Fox Trot or the Rumba from the young and charming Edward Garrett. He was charismatic and interesting. Not that Edward was a choirboy by any means. He had his faults, and by many accounts, lots of them. It was rumored he had a few affairs with several of the high society women – discretely of course. There was even talk he had been married several times but they had failed leaving brokenhearted women in the wake. Those were of course, unsubstantiated rumors. Nothing that could actually be proven. But Edward Garrett was a man to align with, and there were many who had tried to win favor in his limited circle of close acquaintances. One of those was the stunning Amanda Kihn. Amanda was a model. In fact she was the model. Her photo graced each newspaper ad of any high fashion store, and she was making a name for herself as a runway model in New York as well. Yes, Amanda Kihn was fashion in Minnesota.

So when Edward proposed to the tall slender model, and she said "yes", well the wedding could be considered the social event of the year. So here in this historic church in downtown Minneapolis, there would be a wedding like no other wedding. It would be the union of dancer and choreographer Edward Garrett and stunning model extraordinaire Amanda Kihn.

Amanda was from an affluent family who would lavish only the best on their only daughter. The parties. The luncheons. The showers. All had to be the best and the most extravagant imaginable. Today would be the culmination of weeks of parties and events. Today would be the wedding. The church was filled. In the front pews, the extended Kihn family nervous but smiling with pride. Behind them, the social elite dressed in their finest and sporting the most magnificent jewels and accessories hoping to impress someone. In the back were the teachers and select few students from the dance studio. They squirmed with uncomfortable annoyance. Annoyed the wedding, which was to start forty-five minutes ago, was still just a crowd listening to loud and monotonous organ music. Over and over again. The same songs droned on. Edward Garrett, known for his tardiness even to important meetings and events, was again late. And for his own wedding no less.

Amanda Kihn was waiting patiently in the back of the church with her father gripping her elbow ready at any moment to make that walk up the aisle as soon as the curly haired Edward made his appearance. Her dress, an expensive gown created by a favorite New York designer was stunning. Its mermaid style shape hugging her lithe body accentuated her model thinness. Her hair, normally curly and long, was pulled up on top of her head with a spray of flowers strategically placed throughout. Her father, a lean male Amanda look alike, was becoming extremely irritated. Amanda was trying to calm him with her naturally cool temperament, but he was pacing and muttering. The bridesmaids were grouped in clusters whispering uncomfortably. The teachers in the back of the sanctuary could hear the commotion and squirmed with each passing moment. They stared back and forth at each other glancing at their watches and sighing as they realized there was absolutely nothing they could do to change this mounting frustration.

Centered in the pew was the overly exaggerated Megan Meeker. Normally her spiked hair was vibrantly red or purple or some other equally noticeable hue. Today, she had smoothed down the spikes to a subdued sleek close to the head do in a calming chestnut brown color. Her lips remained a vibrant red, but complimented her stylish blah beige dress with a flowing circle skirt. She looked very businesslike and crisp. It was somewhat uncharacteristic of her normal exaggerated style which was always very eye catching and colorful.

Next to her was Carson Hunter wearing his usual gray vest and gray dress pants in a slightly darker shade. The women of the studio had frequently threatened to burn the "usual gray vest" but never succeeded in getting it off of his slight frame. Not that Carson was by any means slender – he was known as the old man of the studio and sported a rounded middle-aged paunch. His dark hair and mustache were neatly trimmed today. They could sometimes get a bit shaggy – a throwback to his days as a tried and true hippy. Carson had begun in the studio not as a seasoned dancer but more as an intellectual. And that sharp mind had gradually developed a stunning and admired dancer. His knowledge of technique was astounding. Dance was a science to Carson Hunter and not just an art form.

Next to Carson was Sydney Monroe and next to her Paddy O'Grady. With a name like Paddy O'Grady, one would assume him to be a red headed freckle faced Irishman. Far from it. Paddy had been adopted as an infant into an American family of Irish decent. He was actually from Korea. So students introduced to their new teacher, Mr. O'Grady were surprised to find a tall, slender Asian with sleek jet black hair and almond shaped eyes. Paddy was known for two things – his muscular physique and his loud booming voice. Paddy O'Grady had slid into the pew next to Sydney much later than the rest of the studio attendees. His schedule was set in stone, and Saturday was one of his workout days. Other than teaching at the studio, his usual haunt was the local gym where he could be seen lifting weights after hours and on weekends. He was well toned and a specimen of good health. His vegetarian diet was supplemented by mounds of wild rice. Each day he could be seen taking long lanky strides into the studio carrying his portable rice maker for his mid-day meal. He smiled at the dark haired Sydney who also served as his current dance partner.

On the other side of Megan Meeker was a tall upright man with a straightforward stare – Jim Peterson. Jim was an engineer who supplemented his education fund with his dancing. Jim was currently enrolled in several classes at the University with the hope of eventually entering a pre-med study. Teaching dance at night allowed him to be a career student. His short wavy black hair and perfect posture made him a study in an ideal dance teacher appearance. Jim could smile – in fact he smiled quite often. Today however, he was thinking about how inconsiderate Edward Garrett was not only to his lovely soon-to-be bride, Amanda but to this entire gathering of people. Jim Peterson was a straight laced conservative in both political and religious views. Not that he forced his opinion on others, but when something wasn't right, it created an unsettled feeling in the pit of his stomach – like right now. He was clearly unsettled. His mouth pursed into an angry sour lemon appearance.

Squeezed in uncomfortably next to Jim Peterson at the end of the row was a new trainee at the studio, Kayla Clark, or as she was known by the staff, "KC". Miss Clark was not your typical dancer. Far from it. She had come in for her original interview with Mr. Garrett with a subdued short hair cut in a sleek black color, subtle make-up, and a conservative navy business suit and matching pumps. No matter that she was a trifle overweight. Mr. Garrett loved a challenge and had immediately made a decision to "whip this one into shape". He had smiled to himself when watching her waddle out the door that first day anticipating the diet and exercise program he would suggest for this new trainee the minute she began her training. But KC had other things in mind. Her second day had been a shock not only for Edward Garrett but for the entire studio staff. She came in with a spiky new hair cut complete with a bleached white color, heavy blue eye shadow that spanned from eyelashes to eyebrows, and a short red clinging dress that hugged her fat rolls around her middle and squeezed her upper arms allowing the bulges of her triceps to hang loosely on her limbs. In addition, she had taken an unhealthy attraction to Carson Hunter. She hadn't been officially invited to the wedding, but had shown up and settled herself at the end of the staff pew taking every possible moment she could to bat her eyes down the row to the silent Carson plunked in the middle of the group.

Ahead of this line of dance teachers were some of the seasoned dance students. Normally, teachers knew the set in stone rule – no fraternizing with the students. Never, never, never. But Edward Garrett had the good sense to know some of these students had been the ones who had made his career what it was, and they deserved to receive an invitation to this special event. So a few rows of mostly gray haired heads could be seen whispering to each other as the time to begin had long ago come and gone. They also had experienced multitudes of tardy appearances by Mr. Garrett, but this was inexcusable. Occasional harsh whispers could be heard from this row as each of the students made their opinions known to the person seated next to them.

Then suddenly as if nothing were amiss, the dashing Edward Garrett appeared at the front of the church in a perfectly cut set of white tails with a stark white dress shirt, matching cummerbund and bow tie. He turned toward the back of the church nodding and smiling broadly at his soon-to-be bride. She in turn rolled her eyes back at him but remained smiling with her thin lips plastered into a pleasant expression. The bridesmaids lined up quickly as if taken by complete surprised when the processional music began to play. Six bridesmaids all looked elegant and not really bridesmaid-y at all in their strapless beaded bodices of pale green above a soft flowing cream skirt meant for dancing and twirling. They carried bouquets of cream flowers with an occasional peach rose poking through and lots of soft greenery to compliment the color of their dresses. They slowly but elegantly strutted down the aisle as if on a fashion show catwalk. Circling around the front of the church, they turned slightly toward the smiling Edward Garrett waiting for the arrival of his bride.

Amanda Kihn was indeed a vision of loveliness. She could never be described as "cute". No, she had a classic look that began with her flowing dark curly hair and moved down to her almost beaked Roman nose and thin lips. Her cheeks were chiseled and hollow accented with just the right amount of color. Although her eyes were not wide-eyed and innocent, they were always artfully made up with that dark smoky look that drew the attention to her features. She had a smoldering look when her make-up was applied. And strangely, she often slipped into the studio completely void of any color to her naturally pale face. Very un-model like indeed.

Amanda's father looked tense and walked straight legged down the aisle alongside his daughter occasionally giving someone seated in the pew a furtive glance and slight smile in recognition. The length of the church must have seemed endless to the poor man at this moment after waiting so long for the presentation of the bride. But he gave her a quick peck on her cheek as he handed her off to her soon-to-be husband. If one looked closely, they might have noticed a glare from Mr. Kihn as the bride slipped her arm into the crooked arm of Edward Garrett. Edward, always the fidgety sort, bounced back and forth between his planted feet and almost seemed to be keeping beat to the processional with his shoulders. It would have been quite humorous if he hadn't made everyone wait so long for this moment.

All in all, the rest of the ceremony went well. Nothing out of the ordinary happened. Despite the hour long delay, everything else was perfect. The receiving line in the front of the church seemed to please both Edward and his new in-laws. They greeted socialite after socialite saluting many with almost kisses on the cheeks and pleasant comments about their lovely attire. "You look wonderful", could be heard over and over even to the wrinkled faces of those who looked as if they were near death's door.

Amanda demurely lowered her eyes and smiled when the studio teachers passed through. They all liked

Amanda – she wasn't in any way snobbish, nor was she catty. She was almost too down to earth for Edward who liked to flaunt his status. Status? That was a joke sometimes. Although he gave the appearance of a wealthy man, in fact he was almost always broke. He was one who liked to show off his toys – an elegant sports car, a pricey condo in the downtown of Minneapolis, classy clothes from Italy, and of course the usual baubles like gold chains and expensive watches. You would think with all of those expensive watches, he could keep time – a common comment from both staff and students. The unfortunate part was Edward might have those toys, but he still hadn't paid for most of them. He had a habit of overspending what he didn't yet have. So although his studio was doing quite well, he always - and always would - live above his means. Did Amanda know about his trait? Megan Meeker had to wonder as she greeted Amanda with a hug and casual peck on the cheek.

The reception was slated for an elegant and posh country club. Mr. Kihn was a member in good standing, and had insisted upon the location. Amanda may have preferred something a bit different, but Edward was thrilled with the choice and the opportunity to gather with the social elite of Minneapolis. There was of course a band – or could it be called an orchestra? Yes. With so many tuxedoed musicians seated in the pit beyond the dance floor, it would most definitely be called an orchestra. The head table was raised above the other attendees and the food and drink was freely flowing. Waiters in smart black suits artfully carried trays of lobster and steak to each table

11

along with bottles of expensive champagne. Edward Garrett loved champagne, and he could be seen frequently refilling his glass with the sparkling bubbly. Amanda floated elegantly between tables greeting friends and relatives, her mermaid skirt swishing gracefully to and fro as she waltzed from place to place. Edward seemed to zero in on the bigwigs – those he knew to be wealthy friends of his in-laws.

Suddenly without warning, the obviously drunk Mr. Kihn sauntered over to Edward Garrett who was busily twirling a stunning socialite decked out in diamonds around the dance floor. Grabbing his shoulder from behind, the slender older man spun Edward to face him and in a slurred voice loudly asked him to step out into the hallway. Edward, who had had as much if not more to drink, looked down his nose at the man and began to laugh – at first a chuckle that quickly to turn into a roaring belly laugh. At the sound of disruption, Amanda turned to look over her shoulder from one of the back tables and her collapsing shoulders said it all. She had been afraid there might be a confrontation between the two men in her life, but she had hoped it wouldn't be tonight.

With swift long strides – as long as a bride in a mermaid style skirt could manage – she reached the two men before any blows could be exchanged and slid between the two. With a glare first at one and then the other, she gripped her father's arms tightly and guided him back to her mother still seated at the head table. With a curt whisper into his ear, she settled him into the seat next to her mom. Collecting her skirt which was no easy task, she returned to Edward and with a cool smile suggested he join her in greeting their guests. The rest of the evening proceeded uneventfully with guests enjoying the orchestra music to dance and toast each other as well as the bride and groom. Mr. Kihn sat glumly at the head table with his wife's hand planted forcefully on his knee. She was a tiny dark haired woman who in no way mirrored her daughter's appearance. Her pale face had only a slight touch of lip color and her obviously dyed hair was cut in a typical older woman style – short and with a perm flowing back from her face in a stiff helmet like do. She wore a linen suit of pale green that matched the bridesmaid bodices and a string of tiny but very exquisite pearls around her lined neck. Amanda's older brother, a younger Mr. Kihn, stood behind the couple with one hand on his father's shoulder and the other clutching tightly to his stemmed champagne glass. His mouth was clenched into an unbecoming scowl.

The next morning the happy couple would travel to Edward Garrett's favorite vacation spot in Puerto Rico. He had developed several dance relationships in the region that proved to be helpful for his choreography. The two of them would stay in a luxurious tourist hotel, but spend some of their time in the local dance studios providing coaching lessons to their students. No doubt it was Edward's way to write off the trip as a tax deduction. Edward definitely wanted to bring his new bride into the dance business. Her reputation as a model would be beneficial for him, and his dance classes would in turn give

Amanda a perfect fitness routine to keep in tip-top shape enhancing her own modeling career.

II.

Megan Meeker sat at the front desk of the studio with her head buried in her hands. She was seated low enough so she could just peek over the top of the reception counter and out the glass door to the entrance of the parking ramp. The studio itself was located at the very bottom of a prominent parking ramp in downtown Minneapolis. So the business people of the downtown area would park their cars each morning, come down the elevator, step out the door and stare directly into the dance studio. Then when they finished work – most likely between four and six each afternoon – they would saunter past the door again planning their evening's entertainment after a hard day in the office. Most mornings Edward and Amanda would spread out across the glistening wooden dance floor with their crew of local models and a few of the dance staff from the studio to exercise. Those tall elegant perfect looking bodies usually brought in scads of new students all hoping to look like the women who tossed their hair carelessly in front of the floor to ceiling mirrors each morning. Or maybe hoping to meet the women who tossed their hair carelessly in front of the floor to ceiling mirrors each morning.

With Edward and the new Mrs. Garrett away for two weeks on their honeymoon, there would be no early morning exercise classes enticing those morning business people to step inside the glass door. Not that that would be a bad thing. Megan knew when Edward was gone, she could sit back and run the dance studio with a bit less stress and worry. Things always seemed to run smoothly when he was away. However, they had just started a new class of teacher trainee candidates, and this next week would be a real headache. She cradled her head gently in her hands rubbing her temple with her forefingers.

When Edward started to date Amanda, he had attempted to include her in studio life by putting her in charge of their training classes. Although Megan loved the down to earth Amanda, letting her lead the training class had been a total disaster. Amanda just knew nothing about the dance business or about ballroom and Latin dancing. With as much talent as Amanda showed dancing with Edward in the morning exercise classes, she was completely clueless as to the proper way to train dancers in the art of ballroom dancing. She would refer to a box step in Waltz for example, as a square. So while a box is certainly a square in geometry, it is not the same in Waltz. Or a turn. She would tell the new trainees to "just spin" without reference to a proper turn or its direction. The trainees and the staff alike soon became frustrated with Amanda's lack of knowledge in this business. So while she certainly could get prospective clients in the door, she was not nor would she ever be a "dance teacher".

Megan glanced back at the dance floor behind her. Jim Peterson was out on the floor with a wedding dance party. There were four people from the same family who had come in for an introductory lesson to prepare them for a cousin's upcoming wedding dance. Jim was his usual tall professional self gathering the four like a mother hen with her chicks. The mother and father clung to each other attempting to learn the proper dance hold, while the daughter – a stunning dark haired beauty of about twenty-three or four stood straight and tall next to her look-a-like brother. The daughter smiled at Jim and made him blush a bit. Megan could see his cheeks flush each time she lowered her dark eyelashes and gave him a grinning stare. The brother was younger and appeared to be totally uninterested in the lesson. Instead, he gazed around the room at the small gathering of trainees waiting for someone to start their time of learning.

Paddy O'Grady was in the corner explaining something to an older student in his booming voice. Megan wondered with rolling eyes if Paddy had a hearing problem that he never noticed his voice carried so loudly around the room. Carson Hunter was sauntering out to the front desk from the hallway carrying his stack of student programs for his day's lessons. Megan glanced at the large sheet of paper propped in front of her and noticed Carson's first student had recently cancelled her lesson rescheduling for the next day.

"Carson," she motioned him toward the desk. "Your student cancelled. Can you teach the training class this hour?"

His expression turned to a sour grimace. "I'll pay you," she begged raising her eyebrows in a pleading expression. Normally teachers were only paid for their teaching lessons to paying students. But she was desperate. She watched the group of three women huddled in the corner – KC, Mary, and Claire. She had to do something with them, and she had another trainee candidate with her mother seated on the reception couch waiting for an interview.

Carson noticed Megan's dilemma and turned his previous distasteful expression to a helpful nod. "What do you want me to work on?" he smoothed his dark mustache gingerly with his fingers.

"Could you review their Fox Trot steps? Basic, basic stuff. Then show them the Rumba and Waltz. Box step with an under arm turn. Both lead and follow, please." He again nodded and continued to saunter out across the dance floor to the three women whispering in the corner. KC was once again in her heavy colorful eye shadow and a short tight purple skirt with a button up white filmy blouse. She smiled gleefully as Carson approached. Mary and Claire were young college student types – preppy skirts and knit tops with long flowing hair pulled to the side with hair clips, and fashionable strappy sandals that would be exceedingly difficult to dance in. They looked all-together different and yet so the same. They blended into the wall; so flat and nondescript in their outward personalities.

Seated across from the reception desk were a young woman of undetermined age and her mother – a woman young enough to pass for the other's sister. She knew they were mother and daughter because they had loudly announced they were there to begin the training class at the suggestion of Amanda Kihn/Garrett. The younger woman was a model. That part of the conversation was announced almost as loudly as Paddy O'Grady was now announcing to his student that they would begin their new pattern in Swing. It fairly boomed across the studio. Megan had directed them to take a seat while she arranged some of the schedules, and they had reluctantly moved to the sofa peering at it first as if they should check first for unwanted bacteria or mold. They were now becoming impatient. The mother began to cross and uncross her legs. Megan lifted the phone receiver and paged back to the teachers' office. "Miss Monroe, could you come up and watch the front desk for me? Morgan is sick today, and I have an interview." She returned the receiver to its proper place and waited for Sydney to scurry up with her arms loaded with paperwork.

"Follow me please to the office," Megan instructed as the mother and daughter duo stood with impatient looks and reluctantly shuffled after her to Mr. Garrett's office door. Edward Garrett's office was right on the corner of the reception area. It had windows facing the dance floor, but normally Edward pulled the heavy curtains so tight, there was no possible way of seeing either in or out of the room. Today, Megan had opened the curtains allowing full view of the dance floor. She motioned for the pair to sit in the overstuffed chairs positioned in front of Edward's large cherry desk as she glanced out at the activities. The two were eager to talk – and brag. Megan soon discovered the daughter, Ashley Dobbs modeled with Amanda. She disliked high school immensely and was considering dropping out to pursue her career in modeling, acting, and of course dance.

The mother gloated as she explained, "Ashley is simply a fabulous dancer, and Amanda thought this would be the perfect stepping stone for a career in the entertainment world. Ashley is really star quality." The mother, Laura nodded her head toward her daughter who settled back in her chair and tossed her head of softly curled caramel colored hair. "I'm a single mom, you see, and not quite able to give my Ashley all of the opportunities she deserves. But Mr. and Mrs. Garrett are. They've promised to take good care of her career and introduce her to the people she needs to meet to hit the big time." Laura Dobbs' speech lapsed from lower class grammatical phrases to a more educated tone. It was hard to determine just where Laura had grown up. She had a slightly Brooklyn accent but then again, seemed so Midwestern. It was a contradiction.

"My training class is fairly new…", Megan began with a slight nod toward the group practicing out the window in a nearby corner of the dance floor with Carson Hunter. Laura drew back and frowned as she placed her hand across her heart. It was as if this group didn't quite meet her standards – or rather the standards of her daughter. Ashley stared out the window and grinned a slow gloating smile. She tilted her chin up slightly changing her look from an innocent schoolgirl appearance to that of a scheming debutant. She shifted slightly in her chair and glanced around the room. Edward had several primitive masks and art pieces from his beloved Caribbean islands as well as a framed photo of himself with Amanda. Both were dressed elegantly – he in a stylish tuxedo and Amanda in a clingy jewel studded evening gown. They both posed for the camera with their arms tightly around each other. Ashley studied the photo closely and lowered her chin with a flash of her hazel eyes.

Laura explained she would be present every evening to watch the training until the Garretts returned from their trip. She was going to make sure the training went along as planned, and Ashley would be in top dance form by the time her mentors came home. Megan tried to explain that ballroom and Latin dancing took longer than the nine or ten days the Garretts would be away, but her explanation seemed to fall on deaf ears. She finally decided to allow Ashley to join the training class already in progress and let the overbearing mother sit in the ballroom to observe. There were small round glass tables and porch style chairs with padded seats around the edge of the ballroom floor. Laura Dobbs could find an empty table and watch the lessons from there. Carson was just finishing up with the three already out on the floor and motioned to Megan as she herded the two to the floor that he needed to get ready for his next lesson. Megan grouped the now four women together and told them to take a short break before resuming their dancing. KC's eyes followed Carson as he left the floor. Her lips parted and closed in a sigh as Megan announced she herself would work with the class from seven till ten that night. Megan's mind began to churn – this would be a long two weeks!

III.

In spite of Megan's initial impressions of Ashley Dobbs as a prima dona, the young Miss Dobbs proved to be a talented dancer. She picked up all the basic patterns quite easily and seemed eager to move on to harder material. But she was a bit overbearing with her personality at times saying things that could easily be construed as insulting to the other members of the training class. There were times when KC and Ashley could easily have pulled each others' hair out if the ballroom hadn't been filled with other people. Particularly when Carson was present. KC seemed reluctant to let Carson Hunter see her as anything but a professional and classy woman at all times. So instead of stooping to Ashley's juvenile behavior of picking a fight with the other trainees, KC simply held her tongue and waited for maybe a better less public time to dig back at this irritation. And Mary and Claire seemed unable to come back with a quick response to Ashley's barbed comments. They seemed to feel it more worthwhile to simply ignore the whole situation. But the two of them became fast friends bonding in their mutual dislike of Ashley Dobbs. At breaks they would scurry to the corner to whisper and discuss topics of unknown subjects.

Megan was in the back teachers' office just before six after about a week of no Edward Garrett when KC stomped into the dingy space that was meant to be a furnace room. Several desks were scattered along the walls and the threadbare carpet showed signs of too much wear with gaping holes visible to trip up a teacher in dance shoes with spiked heels if not careful.

"Miss Clark, you are not yet allowed in the teachers' office," Megan announced as KC twirled in an attempt to spot Carson Hunter. Carson hadn't yet come back from lunch – lunch was late for teachers who taught from one in the afternoon until ten at night.

"I know. I know." KC's pale white skin looked especially ghost-like in the darkness of the teachers' office. "I just need to let off some steam. I can hardly stand another hour, another minute with that pompous Miss Dobbs. She is about as irritating as a chipmunk running in front of a caged lion." KC could be very humorous at times Megan decided. The chipmunk was exactly the correct description of Ashley Dobbs. "And that mother of hers! She is definitely a bit nutty."

"Now why do you say that?" Megan had hardly noticed Laura Dobbs at all this past week. The woman had been quietly seated at a back table with never any conversation with anyone in the studio as far as Megan could determine.

"She looks at you – or rather at me – as if I don't deserve to be in the same room as her precious daughter.

It's as if the rest of us aren't good enough to be in the training class with her. It's so patronizing!" KC rolled her eyes and huffed. Her lower lip extended into a quick pout.

"She is a good dancer...," Megan was trying to spark more information. A look was not really a factual strike against someone's actual opinion.

"Of course she's a good dancer," KC glared. "She's been in dance classes since she was three years old. And without any charge to the dear Miss Laura Dobbs, I might add."

"What do you mean by that?" Megan tilted her head for a closer focus on KC.

"She brags all the time that she has maneuvered teachers and studios to give her daughter instruction for free. And that includes everything else like her portfolio for modeling and even her clothes. She gives them a sob story about their sad existence, and they get anything they want free of charge. That just doesn't seem fair for the rest of us who actually have to work for what we've gotten." KC was crisp and clear in making her accusations.

"Are you sure of this?" Megan frowned.

"Absolutely. Just ask her yourself if you don't believe me," KC puffed up her already ample chest and strutted back out the door like a peacock proud and determined.

Megan Meeker laid her head down on her desk. Why do these things happen whenever Edward is gone? Just when it seems they'll have an easy and uncomplicated week without him, why do things always go terribly wrong? Her teeth clutched tightly into a guttural growl.

Jim Peterson hurried through the door and gently sat his black leather schedule folder on his perfectly neat desk on the other side of the spacious furnace room. He took off his suit jacket and carefully hung it on the back of his chair before sitting down and restraightening his already straight desktop. He flipped open his leather folder and traced down the list along the side of his calendar for his to do list. Carefully, he lifted the phone receiver and dialed the number under his finger. "May I speak to Miss Annie St. Germaine, please? Hello? Miss St. Germaine? This is Mr. James Peterson from the dance studio. We had a lesson the other evening, and I am just calling to schedule our second lesson."

Megan smiled as she listened to Jim. He was always so professional in his approach to his students. It was a pleasure listening to him after the conversation a moment ago with KC. Jim Peterson followed every studio rule by the book and there were never any problems with Jim or with his students. Now she had a whole class of trainee headaches. How was she going to deal with these people?

The evening was trying, but Megan managed to ignore the problems successfully. Yes, KC looked like a sausage about to burst in her clinging peach colored mini

24

sheath and three inch wedged penny loafers. Her hair was even more vibrant white than usual and her deep blue eye shadow scary. Claire and Mary seemed to fasten themselves to each other like Siamese twins avoiding the other two trainees at all cost. Ashley Dobbs managed to turn her nose up at all of the other trainees as well as the other teachers and students as she practiced her patterns alone in the corner asking to take her certification test "early, if possible." Her proud mother, Laura lounged at the corner table with a much too satisfied grin on her face when Ashley began asking the questions about early certification. Yes, tonight was a nightmare but Megan Meeker left the studio at ten minutes after ten with a satisfaction that she had successfully dodged the bullet and prayed Edward Garrett would return soon.

The next day Ashley Dobbs pranced in followed by her mother almost bursting with news. Her long hair was tied up on the side in a stylish tail and her hollowed cheeks slightly tinted. She must have had a show or photo shoot today. Her wrapped skirt flapped opened to show a bit of leg as she leaned down to slip off her flat sandals and slide her feet into new Latin dance sandals of a shimmering nude tone with a high three inch heel. Glancing up, she noticed Megan staring at her new purchase.

"Actually, Amanda called today and suggested I buy these," she gloated with a flashing smile. "Her treat, of course," she added with a snip. "Oh, and they told me to let you know they'll be back this evening."

Megan's lips tightened. She was getting news about her boss from one of her trainees. What next? Laura Dobbs stood behind her daughter with a flippant grin as if to let Megan know who was really in charge. Laura's thin body seemed a bit gaunt tonight as Laura played restlessly with her blouse buttons. Was it her coloring or did her clothes seem to hang on her a little more loosely than usual?

Megan leaned over the reception desk and addressed mother Dobbs. "And exactly what do you do, Laura? I mean for a job and all. You seem to have a flexible schedule to come every day to the studio with Ashley and all?" Megan tried to phrase her question as just a curiosity rather than an interrogation.

Laura hesitated but didn't seem offended by the question at all. "Actually, I am on disability. So I don't work at all," she smiled as if she had pulled a fast one on someone. It was almost a statement of pride.

"Oh," Megan continued. "I'm sorry you are injured. What happened?"

This time Laura hesitated. "I just had a little accident a few years ago. But it doesn't really bother me too much now," she frowned and bit her lip. "The lawsuit took care of all my medical bills pretty well." Her eyes glinted like a cat that caught the mouse. Maybe KC's assessment of their studio conversations was not as far off as Megan had first suspected. Maybe these two Dobbs were indeed about to take the studio for a free ride just like they appeared to have done with other studios.

Ashley scurried out to the dance floor to try out her new shoes. They appeared to be working well as Ashley spun in front of the mirror posing to check out her own image tipping her chin and pursing her lips to create a model image as the end of each turn. She rubbed the bottoms of the shoes on the floor as if to get a better feel of their use. The dance shoes had the typical suede bottoms moving smoothly along the wooden floor. The others in the training class sauntered in and stared at the dance shoes. With a gloating smile, Ashley was quick to explain who had paid for her new dance shoes. Just another little tidbit the group could hold against their fellow trainee.

Megan sat at the desk and stared at the daily teaching schedule to see who would be free to work with the training class tonight when the light tinkling on the door sounded to announce a visitor. She waited a moment and then looked up to see Edward and Amanda Garrett with their arms wrapped around each other smiling out toward the dance floor as if to say "Home!" Amanda looked refreshed and healthy with an excitement she hadn't shown during their engagement. It was a feeling of calm - tan feeling of calm. Edward was his usual energetic and bouncy self. His curly hair – actually a wig or rather toupee – fit snuggly on his head giving him a more youthful appearance than his actual real self. He actually appeared to be more of a Bozo the clown without it. As usual, he fingered the edges adjusting it even though it didn't need adjusting. He wore more casual attire than he normally wore into the studio – always requiring professional clothing from his staff. Tonight he carried his suit bag over his shoulder wearing a brightly printed Caribbean short sleeve shirt with a pair of expensive jeans and slip on shoes. Amanda had on a printed sun dress with a geometric pattern in yellows and teals. She had a pair of strappy sandals that wrapped up her slender calves criss crossing to her knees. She waved to Ashley Dobbs who squealed excitedly and scampered off toward the pair in a horse-like galloping lope.

"Do you like them?" Ashley asked displaying her new dance shoes. She tipped her foot to each side for better inspection. Both Amanda and Edward nodded their approval as they each gave her a hug. "Do you want to see me dance in them?" Ashley asked in a little girl tone of voice.

"Of course, dear." Amanda nodded and acknowledged Laura seated across the room at the small round glass table. Laura smiled weakly and lifted a finger - a small display of greeting. Then she looked down at the table as if contemplating the waves of glass in the surface. Megan Meeker frowned at the strange behavior. Why wouldn't she get up and go speak with the Garretts? Why did she seem to sit back in the corner and let Ashley take center stage? Suddenly Laura seemed weak and almost helpless.

Amanda and Edward stepped to the edge of the dance floor and watched Ashley go through her dance patterns. She grinned back proudly at them. Amanda was encouraging with a few quick claps after each pattern was completed. Edward was giving her a clowning smile – all teeth – then grabbed Sydney Monroe as she walked off the floor from a lesson and began to spin her into a fast Cha Cha. The music was beating with a Latin rhythm and the two began with a cross over to walk around turn into a swivel with pull back. Ashley suddenly found her face frozen – her grin turned to a twist of jealousy. She was trying to show her progress to Edward and expected his complete attention and excitement at her ability then he grabs another and proceeds to humiliate her with a spectacular dance demonstration.

He stopped dancing spun Sydney Monroe over to the side of the floor and sauntered over to where Ashley stood. "That's what you will look like in a few months with lots of nightly practice," he stated and glanced over for approval from Amanda. Amanda licked her lips nervously. She had noticed the change in Ashley's demeanor when Edward began the demonstration and was considering what she could do to remedy the situation.

"You know, Edward," Amanda suggested with a quick sweetness to her voice. "If Ashley comes in every morning to rehearsal with us she would show faster improvement and possibly be a show partner for you in …what…a few short weeks, maybe?" Amanda had been trying to find a dance partner for Edward for quite some time now. She knew how much dancing and performing meant to Edward. Maybe this was a perfect solution to the problem.

Ashley turned to face Amanda with a new hopeful look in her face. She waited - waited for more. Her chin jutted forward as if she anticipated Amanda to speak again. Amanda was quiet. Edward was quiet. The room was still, a quiet echo.

Amanda took a deep breath and hoped Edward would agree with her assessment, but he seemed oblivious to what was expected. So Amanda faced Ashley directly and took her by the shoulders. "Ashley, dear, you are like our own daughter." She smiled and then in a quiet whisper added, "We know your mother is ill and can't care for you the way someone of your talents should be cared for. We will care for you as if we were your own flesh and blood parents and give you every opportunity to be a successful model and dancer." Amanda smiled warmly, and Ashley smiled sweetly back. That was what she wanted to hear. She melted into Amanda's arms with a grateful sigh and stared over at Edward who seemed supportive of his new wife's decision to "adopt" a seventeen year old as their new "child".

Megan proceeded to introduce Edward – and Amanda – to the remaining members of the new training class. "You remember Miss Clark, KC we call her," she began pulling the startled woman into the intimate circle in the middle of the floor. Edward stepped back and stared. "I don't think you look the same as when I last saw you," he frowned as if trying to pinpoint the change.

"No," she announced boldly. "I dyed my hair." She stroked the new spiky hairdo proudly. "I thought I needed a little spice as a new dancer in this fine establishment."

Edward was speechless. He opened his mouth to make a comment and then quickly shut it again. He nodded as if to agree but Megan could see the shock in his eyes so she continued. "And this is Claire and Mary here." She almost pushed the two women in Edward's direction and each nodded politely. "I know you like us to be more professional by addressing our teachers by their last names, but these are new trainees, and we're getting to that next in the training." Edward didn't pay much attention to Megan's babbling. He was too stunned by his new "daughter" and his other white haired trainee in her mint green mini skirt and matching vest.

Amanda was describing the morning rehearsals in detail to a giddy Ashley Dobbs and painting a picture about the performances in her future. "The costumes are fabulous," she was saying. "I personally purchase only the best for Edward and his partners." Amanda was laying it on thick portraying a rosy portrait of the fabulous potential of a dance career for Ashley Dobbs.

As Ashley and her mother left the studio with Edward and Amanda for the evening, Megan Meeker once again sat behind the reception desk staring after the small group as they headed out for a late dinner. Sydney Monroe leaned on the top of the desk and asked, "What was happening tonight that I had to dance with Edward?"

Megan shook her head. "All I know is Amanda and Edward Garrett adopted a seventeen year old girl who already has a mother who seems perfectly healthy when she comes in here but has somehow convinced the Garretts that she is deathly ill. What does that all mean?"

"It means it's going to cost the studio money, and we'll all somehow suffer," Sydney evaluated in a voice that was crisp and to the point.

"I think you are right," Megan sighed. "Home?"

"I'll race you to the bus stop," Sydney snatched her purse and held the door for Megan to follow.

IV.

The next few weeks were quite uneventful. Amanda and Edward home after the wedding and honeymoon seemed surprisingly calming for the studio and the staff. Ashley joined the Garretts and the models who attended the morning exercise sessions. Amanda made Ashley her special project, and the girl seemed to thrive with the attention. Laura Dobbs didn't come in to the studio any more. Amanda herself dropped off Ashley for her evening training sessions. The improvement in Ashley's dancing was quite evident just as Amanda had predicted.

One particularly quiet evening, Edward called Megan into his office for a brief meeting about the upcoming teacher tests. Teachers in each region took yearly tests in dancing skills, teaching, and dance knowledge. Some years they had traveled to Milwaukee.

Sometimes it was to Chicago. But this year it would be here in Minneapolis. They would host the annual tests at one of the hotels able not only to accommodate all of the studios' staff but the tests themselves in their spacious ballrooms. Megan dreaded the event as she would be the one to handle arrangements. It was just a lot more work piled on to her already hectic schedule.

"I know it's expensive, but I think we should book rooms for all of our teachers to stay directly in the hotel itself," Edward was saying as he began to ponder some of the details Megan needed to attend to. "After all, we are the hosts. And," he added, "most of our teachers don't drive. There would be transportation issues if they had to come and go for all of the evening activities."

Megan nodded. She knew this to be true. She added the item to her long To Do list.

"Can you have the staff prepared for their tests?" he asked with a frown. He never wanted his staff to be second to any other studio. He expected the best. Megan nodded. "And can you have the trainees ready as well?"

At this Megan cringed. She had also anticipated this request. Edward had been pushing her to get this group ready to teach, no doubt because he wanted Ashley Dobbs to be more enthusiastic about her career in the studio. Both he and Megan had noticed her bored expressions when dancing with the other trainees each evening. He certainly didn't want her to opt out of the studio now that she was partnering with him for shows. No, he wanted her enthusiastically participating as a full staff member. He was about to ask another question when there was a slight rap on his door. The heavy door blocked the appearance of the person who wished entrance, so he motioned for Megan to answer the knock.

Standing at the door laden down with costume bags was Amanda. "Sorry," she profusely apologized. "I don't want to interrupt, but it is extremely important I speak with Edward." She glanced past Megan and smiled sweetly at her husband who of course motioned her in. He stood to wrap an arm around her shoulders and give her a peck on the cheek although the added weight of his arm seemed to make her struggle with her bags all the more. She draped everything over the back of one of the chairs and began her explanation for this sudden visit.

"My agent just called and offered me an opportunity to do a couple of New York fashion shows," she began before Megan could escape the room. The door remained ajar, and she caught the rest of the conversation – eavesdropping just a tiny bit of course.

"I don't have much time," Amanda continued. "I leave tonight. It's only for three weeks – a month tops. I'll call you every night and tell you how the shows go. It's just such a fabulous opportunity for me. I've been waiting for years to do this, and it is finally becoming a reality. What a boost for my career! Sorry, darling. I know you'll take good care of Ashley. Make sure she gets to all of the morning rehearsals. I'll check on her progress. I have little time to say good-by to anyone. So can you let her know about all of this for me?" Her breathless banter was met with a surprised but supportive nod from Edward Garrett after an initial pouting session. Evidently they had discussed the possibility of such an opportunity, and he was trying to take the news with a quiet calm although he had his usual nervous pumping of his legs as he sat in his desk chair. After a moment of pondering, he stood and with outstretched arms engulfed his wife with a big hug and lingering kiss on the lips.

"I'm off to the airport now. My taxi is waiting out front. I knew you would understand the quickness of my decision. When a model in one of these shows cancels, there is no time to ponder the idea of taking her spot. It's either a yes or no. And I hate to admit it, but I'm no teenager anymore." Her voice was matter of fact and decisive. Edward managed a grin and an "I'll miss you," as he helped her carry her bags to the yellow cab outside the door never arguing or debating her age assessment.

"Do well! And have fun," he waved as the taxi squealed away from the curb. Then he went inside the studio to tell Ashley of Amanda's departure. At first Ashley seemed to react with anger. Was she angry that Amanda was leaving – that Amanda hadn't had time to say good-by herself – or that Amanda had the opportunity and Ashley herself hadn't? It was hard to say, but her anger was quite evident for the rest of the evening. She seemed to mope about the dance floor with no interest in practicing her patterns. Even when Edward came out to the floor and tried to dance with her, she had been hesitant and standoffish. In the end, Edward seemed to almost plead with her. He led her into his office for a little chat that was still in session when the rest of the staff finally called it a day and left.

Strangely, by the next morning, Ashley Dobbs seemed pleasant and almost uncharacteristically cheerful. Edward must have promised something – just like a doting father would when trying to win back the good graces of a favorite daughter. Maybe he could be a good parent after all.

Edward announced to the staff that day about the testing dates and had Megan review what would be expected. Then he proudly announced he and Ashley Dobbs would be featured dancers in the annual downtown parade that weekend. The downtown main street was a buses only route during the week and would be used for the summer parade route this weekend. He and Ashley would be on top of a float dancing to the music provided by a small Latin band seated at the back of the float. Ashley seemed pleased and giddy with the announcement although it was evident she already knew about the event.

"Megan, do we have an appropriate costume Ashley could wear? I think Amanda has some of her dresses hanging in the costume closet. Could you select something for her?" Edward turned toward Megan, and she again took another note. She nodded with little emotion to the request. "We'd love to have all of you attend and cheer us on. This is Ashley's first performance after all. Support each other

– you know…one big happy family!" Edward babbled with a nervous titter in his voice.

Might just be fun, Megan thought as she searched through the closet after the meeting ended. The closet was packed with dresses and men's tuxedos accumulated over the years. Yes, Amanda had placed a few of her dresses in with the other items. Megan pulled these out. Each dress was lovely and made for someone extremely slender and tall. Ashley had a model-like frame, but was not nearly as thin and angular as Amanda. Amanda was almost six feet tall and Ashley was a shorter five eight or nine. Some of the skirts would sweep the ground if Ashley tried to wear them. But Megan picked out a floating white halter dress with a handkerchief cut skirt that might work out perfectly for the parade. It was wispy and would make the cantankerous Ashley look like an angel. Megan packed the other dresses back into the closet and let the dress hang out, smoothing down some of the wrinkles from the tight quarters of the closet.

Ashley meandered by in her new dance shoes and spotted the dress. She cocked her head to the left and back to the right then grasped the skirt to feel the material. Megan peered over the reception desk watching her reaction. Ashley frowned and shook the bottom of the skirt.

"It's made to twirl just perfectly," Megan chirped. "Amanda picked it especially for a dance performance. So it will work out just fine for your show."

"Humpf," Ashley snorted yanking open the closet door and flipping through the other dresses packed tightly into the small space. She gripped the hanger of a slinky sequined dress low cut in the front and backless. It hung off the hanger in a long narrow line.

"Too long for you and too revealing in the front. It will fall right off of you on your first turn," Megan offered with a snap.

Ashley turned and glared at Miss Meeker then snatching the dress from its hanger went to the restroom to try it on. She pranced back out to the reception area with the hem of the dress trailing along the floor behind her. The sleek sequined number clung to her body squeezing in tightly around her thighs. Paddy O'Grady following her down the hall announced loudly in his booming voice, "Can't dance in that!" Then he grasped her hand and twirled her out to the dance floor as the strap on the right shoulder slipped off revealing a tiny breast. But Paddy continued to spin her wrapping her new dance shoes into the skirt creating a tornado effect of fabric around her calves causing her to lilt to the left until she fell flat on the floor. "Certainly won't work on a float with all of that movement. You'll be lucky if you can stay on with a proper fitting dress!" he again announced in his loud echoing voice. Megan snickered, and Ashley flounced off in a huff after he offered a hand to help her up to a standing position and tried unsuccessfully to unwrap her mummified legs. She finally had to pull the whole dress up to her hips and waddle off with everything cinched around her waist.

Megan smiled and went back to her schedule and paperwork. When she looked up again, the white halter dress was gone – and so was Ashley Dobbs.

Saturday was a warm but blustery day. The wind was whipping the few slender trees planted along the parade route into a whistling choir. Megan found Carson and KC sitting at an outdoor café and ordered a cold beer. They were munching on chips and cheese and chitchatting about studio gossip. KC seemed to know everything about everyone, and in spite of Carson's normal "who cares" attitude, he seemed to be taken in by the bits of news she was sharing. Megan sat back in her chair to enjoy the bustle of the street crowds trying to find suitable places to view the parade and sipped her frosty beer. It was a relaxing warm day in spite of the sometimes violent breeze. Occasionally she found she had to cling to her napkin to keep it from whipping out from under her mug. It was that kind of day.

"And those two," KC was saying. "I don't know what is going on with little Miss Mary and tag along Claire, but they have secrets. What could be so sensitive that they can't share it with everyone else? I tell you those two are strange!"

Megan chuckled. Talk about calling the kettle black. KC was wearing over the knee black shiny boots with soles that had to be three inches thick and short hot pants in a clown striped yellow and purple with a laced up leather vest in vibrant orange. Her hair was especially spiky today and when the wind blew, it seemed to halo around her plump face accentuating her purple eye shadow that gave her the appearance of someone who had two black eyes. Strange? There couldn't be much stranger than Kayla Clark on this particular day. Carson Hunter seemed intrigued by the woman. They chatted and laughed and chomped on chips as the parade began with a high school band in the lead. The drum major twirled his staff and high stepped down the street with the uniformed musicians swinging back and forth to the beat of the drums. They all sported tall hats with golden plumes. The plumes waivered back and forth as the wind flicked causing the children who were squeezed along the curb to fling their heads back and forth in matching rhythm.

A few colorful clowns with big noses and even bigger wigs frolicked down the street tossing wrapped candy at the screaming children. Balloons bobbed wildly up and down with the carriers trying desperately to hang on to their strings. Every so often one got away and began to drift higher and farther away from the skyscraping buildings of the downtown proper until they were only tiny dots among the clouds.

Finally the beat of the Latin band could be heard in the distance, and Megan tapped KC and Carson's arms to wait and watch for the studio float. They could see it turning the corner a few blocks away. Edward Garrett, tall and vibrant in a silky white shirt and white dress pants stood out as the float came closer. Ashley Dobbs seemed to be clinging for dear life to her partner who was trying desperately to spin her. But she only clung tighter, her white skirt floating up and down revealing panties – a lacy pair of bikinis.

"Didn't anyone tell her about dance pants?" Megan groaned. "She can't be that stupid!"

Edward's face was becoming more and more distorted and fierce as he attempted to perform his choreographed dance with a stick straight wailing girl. It was quite embarrassing. Megan wanted to hide her head in her hands, but continued to watch in horror as it got worse. At one point, Edward almost managed to push Ashley off the float completely, but she managed to grasp onto his arm and cling on for dear life. She somehow got her feet situated back onto the bed of the float and sat right down holding on to the edge with all of her might and a fierce look of contempt in her eyes. Not a pretty picture. Not a pretty first dance experience.

Megan finished the last swig of her beer and raced – well, walked quickly – down the street attempting to follow the path of the float for a better look at the situation. She dodged and weaved between people, managing to almost catch up to the float that was now rocking back and forth from side to side tossing the pair from one edge to the other. In addition to the gusts of wind and the rocky ride, big drops of rain had begun to fall. A small dark cloud seemed to perch itself directly over the float, and now the dancers were getting wet. By the time the parade route ended, Ashley Dobbs was a drenched mess. Her hair was plastered to her head, her heavy stage make-up dripping down her cheeks, and her dress clinging in an unforgiving

41

manner to her young body. Of course as soon as the float reached the end of the route, the rain stopped and a bit of yellow sun streamed golden beams through the wet handkerchief cut skirt. Ashley Dobbs stomped off twisting and turning on her ruined new dance shoes in the direction of the studio.

"I wonder if this is the last time we see that young lady," Megan sighed as KC and Carson pulled up behind her to catch a glimpse of the performance ending. Carson stroked his mustache as KC draped a plump arm over his shoulder.

Much to everyone's surprise, Monday morning Ashley Dobbs was back in the studio all smiles with no comments on her Saturday performance. Maybe she didn't even realize anyone from the studio had witnessed the disaster. If she did, she made no comment. But she had on a brand new pair of strappy Latin dance sandals and a new zest for her dancing.

Megan Meeker ran down her list of preparation for the dance testing crossing off each item as it came and left. Things were beginning to gel, and she was feeling a little less stressed as the weekend event was approaching. In all of her delight as she realized the list was growing considerably shorter, she had the sinking feeling she was missing something – something that was very important. What could it be? Rooms booked. Check. Information sent out and received from studios and judging panels. Check. Teachers practicing patterns and simulations for tests. Check. Meals selected from the hotel menus.

Check. Schedule checked and rechecked. Awards ordered and ready to go. Check. Music selected for testing and evening dance. Check. What was missing? Oh, my. She had a sudden flash what wasn't on the list. The staff routine. Edward Garrett always insisted his staff present a routine at every regional event. It was his rule, and a rule that was never, ever broken. He loved to show off his staff of teachers as the best in the area. It was only a few days until the testing was to take place, and they had nothing prepared!

Megan dreaded the confrontation. She would have to tell Edward, and his reaction would not be pleasant. With Amanda gone and his new father duties, Edward himself had probably forgotten the routine as well. But it was certain he would put the blame on Megan for the oversight. She dragged herself over to his enormous heavy office door and rapped lightly.

"Come in," came back the pleasant response. Never a good sign. He was cheerful.

Megan peeked in and saw Edward lounging in his comfy chair with his feet propped on his desk. His Italian loafers of soft leather were long and narrow with the soles hardily scuffed.

"I hate to be the bearer of bad news," Megan began, "but we have no staff routine for the testing this weekend." Her words dragged uncomfortably.

"No need to worry," Edward Garrett replied cheerfully. "Ashley and I will be performing a fabulous Mambo routine. It will absolutely knock your socks off!" He was glowing…and happy. How strange! After the disaster at the parade, how could he be so confident in this "fabulous Mambo routine"? He was not a man who praised a routine if it wasn't just that – "fabulous". Megan shrugged and turned to leave. This new development made her a bit curious and heightened her anxiety for the upcoming weekend.

V.

The hotel was elegant. Megan Meeker carrying her garment bag had arrived early to check all arrangements for a final time. Dancers would be arriving shortly from the other states and would be expecting everything to be in order for a prompt beginning to what would be an interesting weekend. Although they had had other events at this particular hotel, she always found her initial entrance to be a truly breathtaking experience. The elegant and plush carpets were not business typical, and the chandeliers glistened with eye catching splendor. The bell staff was dressed in crisp navy and gold uniforms and stood at attention waiting for any order to serve. The front desk attendant was smiling a greeting and cheerfully nodded as Megan approached briskly walking as if she knew just where she was going. And she did. The ballrooms were just beyond the front desk and the sleep rooms scattered throughout the four upper floors. Megan would be rooming with Sydney, KC with Ashley, and of course Mary with Claire. Paddy would be with Carson as Jim Peterson had several university classes he couldn't possibly miss. So he would not stay in the hotel, but would commute back and forth as his schedule permitted. Of course, Edward would have his own suite. He always expected something lush and large so he could easily entertain throughout the weekend. He would expect his own staff and the owners of the other studios to attend the cocktail parties he would host each evening. It was tradition.

After picking up her room key and the other keys for the rest of the staff members, Megan passed the ballrooms peeking in to make sure tables were set properly. She had sent over a floor plan with the arrangement. Everything looked to be in order. A table of coffee urns and water pitchers were set in the corner along with a display of pastries and muffins. The travelers would be hungry when they arrived. Most had driven through the night in order to get to the hotel for the opening meeting at nine am. She scampered by the table and snatched a blueberry muffin on the way to her room checking her watch carefully as she waited for the elevator. Her room was nice – two queen sized beds divided by a night stand. It was a typical arrangement but very comfortable. As soon as the district director arrived and took over, Megan would feel relieved. Her duties would end, and she could enjoy the weekend. She no longer had to go through the testing and had opted out as a judge. The weeks of stressful worry would soon be over. She smiled as she hung up her garment bag and grabbed the remote to check out the channels. Flopping on the bed, she would wander back down to the ballroom in about fifteen minutes or so to greet the other dancers when they arrived.

Megan was wearing a bright red dress with a wide matching belt and full skirt. It was her trademark attire to be vibrant and very visual. She would not disappoint today. Her hair was fluffed and her lipstick a match with her dress. As the other studio managers and owners arrived, they made a bee line to Megan to give her a hug and kiss on the cheek. "You look lovely, darling," or "Sweetheart, what a lovely dress" would be repeated all morning as the dancers arrived. Megan reveled in the attention. However, when KC arrived in her lime green mini skirt and peasant blouse, some of the attention seemed to shift. Not overshadowing Megan, but more as a distraction. KC was very visible that was certain. After the initial shock wore off, most just ignored the trainee and began to focus on their own staff members circling tables and grabbing coffee in preparation for the assignments and instructions on the testing.

Edward had not yet arrived. Although it was no surprise, Megan was irritated. The regional director was waiting to begin the meeting until he arrived as the host owner. Megan finally leaned over to suggest they start without him. True to form, half way through the instructions, Edward Garrett with a giddy Ashley Dobbs following behind arrived with a flourish. Not satisfied to slide in quietly, the two of them made a grand entrance that promptly stopped the meeting and forced the director to suggest a brief break for coffee and water refills. Megan sighed and rolled her eyes. Edward was smartly dressed in a cream colored suit with matching tie and a pale teal dress shirt. Ashley looked every bit the little girl she was in a flouncy peasant skirt and low cut top that revealed she had nothing to reveal. She clutched her dance sandals in hand and dropped a small purse on a front table claiming her spot.

When the meeting resumed, the director announced they would be divided into four groups. Group one would go to dance testing, two to teaching presentation, three to written test, and four to group dance. Then they would switch. The groups were divided into dance levels so the one attending the group dance could do their certification testing with others who were at their same dance level. That meant the four groups would have two testing in the Bronze level, one in the Silver and one in the Gold level. Very organized, thought Megan as she nodded approvingly of the plan. Names were read off as to group assignments, and they were off. Megan calmly grabbed a nice hot cup of coffee with plenty of cream and settled herself out in the lobby preferring not to watch the dance tests. She watched the groups shift from one room to another and observed the interaction of the dancers with each other – discussing the difficulty of the test they just took.

She took a sip of her coffee as another studio manager plopped himself down into one of the exquisitely patterned overstuffed chairs. "So what's with this young thing tagging along with Edward?" he quipped as he settled in to watch the parade of teachers change rooms. Everyone in the dance business with any experience knew each other quite well. "Where's Amanda?" he frowned. "Don't tell me the marriage is over already."

"No," Megan laughed. "She's in New York doing a bit of modeling. It's a good boost for her career. It's just for a few weeks. The girl is sort of their 'adoptee'."

"What?" the manager quickly snapped his head toward Megan for further information.

"She's a young model with a shabby home life that Amanda has taken under her wing. She thinks Ashley would be a good partner for Edward – dancing that is." Megan explained the situation in short but to the point sentences.

"Well, they seem to be more than just partners if you ask me," the manager commented as one of his teachers signaled wildly for him to help her. He jumped to his feet and scampered off to see what the issue was. "Always something …", he muttered as he strode across the lobby with long quick steps and a signaling wave toward the ballroom.

Megan didn't like other managers and dancers getting the wrong impression of Ashley Dobbs. She did appear to be too much of a shadow and not very independent as the day continued. She seemed glued to Edward's side and determined to attach herself to his every move.

At the end of the afternoon there was an awards ceremony. Not like the other ceremonies held in past years where there were scores and teams chosen to receive acknowledgement. Instead they provided certificates for the teachers who had passed their dance tests and were now certified in their various levels. Megan's teachers were clearly excited to receive their certification. It meant a pay raise for each one who passed. Raises were the responsibility of the teacher and not the opinion of management. It was quite a fair system that placed the financials squarely on the shoulder of the employee – never a reason for questions.

There would be an evening banquet and dance after awards, but the hotel staff needed time to reset all of the tables and arrange for the evening's festivities. So the dancers were shooed out the door to go to their rooms or meet for cocktails in the hotel bar. Megan stood in the lobby watching the groups make decisions – where, when and so forth. The Minneapolis staff decided to change clothes and meet in the lobby for a drink before dinner. So Megan and Sydney took the elevator to their room. It was down the hall from the other staff rooms. They spotted Mary and Claire marching arm in arm to their room, and KC chit chatted with Carson as they ambled down to their rooms which happened to be next door to each other.

"What are you going to wear?" Sydney plopped down on her bed and leaned back onto a stack of pillows as she flipped on the TV.

"I brought two outfits because I couldn't decide." She held up a light pink dress with a stoned bodice and scalloped hem. Then she pulled out a silk green pantsuit – three pieces in a shimmering green jeweled tone.

"I vote on the green," Sydney pointed at the second outfit. "I'm wearing my usual little black dress. I have nothing else." She sighed.

"And it is very lovely indeed," Megan smiled encouragingly. "With a little necklace or some dangling earrings, it will look stunning."

Megan carried the green suit into the bathroom and shortly came out to stare into the mirror. Yes, the jacket draped elegantly in pointed peaks almost to her knees. Her pants sleekly flowed to the tip of her golden dance sandals. The lines of the outfit were indeed gorgeous. Yes, it would be perfect for the evening.

Sydney had already slipped into her black dress – sleeveless with a V neckline. She had piled her hair up into a side ponytail and was holding up a pair of dangling gold filament earrings to her earlobes to see if they might add to the outfit. "Yes?"

"Yes," Megan nodded. "Perfect. And you are right, this outfit works."

Sydney put in the earrings and after a second look at herself announced, "Let's head out, shall we?"

The two of them stepped out into the hallway and headed toward the elevator. The lobby and bar was crowded with dancers, all dressed to the nines in slinky dresses and classy dress shirts. They found two stools at the edge of the bar and waited for the rest of the group. Megan signaled for a white wine, and Sydney ordered a cold beer.

Soon Carson had joined them along with Paddy. Paddy was his usual loud self greeting dancers from the other studios with quick jab to the arm or a point of the finger. Megan and Sydney circled in toward each other to sip their drinks.

"Oh, my God!" KC was practically bursting at the seams as she scurried across the bar floor toward the small group huddled in the corner. "It was unbelievable!" She shook her head furiously and leaned in toward Carson who was resting his elbow on the bar nursing a rum and coke. Carson cocked his head to the side and waited for the chatter to begin. He was getting used to her. With her eyes wide as saucers, KC tossed her white spiky hair to and fro. Her eyes were rimmed with sparkling lavender eye shadow and her cheeks circled in hot pink blush. She wore a longer than usual skirt in a purple satin with a wide patterned sash and a low cut white top revealing ample breasts. "So I'm changing in the bathroom and after looking gorgeous," she lifted a tantalizing shoulder and rolled it before continuing. "When I come out to the room, there is Ashley Dobbs," she put her hands on her hips and pursed her lips.

"Of course there is Ashley Dobbs," Megan stated flatly sipping her wine. "She's your roommate."

"Yes, yes. She's my roommate… but there she is with no top on – and she has nothing to be proud of, I must say. Standing in front of her is Mr. Garrett. They are arguing. Ashley is telling him she is not going with him to his room. She's standing there topless and then she sees me and crosses her arms over her chest. She actually hides her breasts from me, but not Eddie G." KC was eager to share every bit of her gossip. She turned to Carson and with an innocent look on her face asked, "What is going on here?"

Megan sighed. "You must be mistaken. Edward would in no way jeopardize his relationship with Amanda. Ashley is simply his prodigy. They are partners. That's all."

KC shrugged. "I know what I saw." She pouted and lowered her eyes toward Carson who was playing with an ice cube in his drink.

"Want something to drink?" Carson whispered as he motioned for the bartender. She nodded back.

When the doors opened allowing the dancers to enter the ballroom, the area had been transformed. The tables were covered with white tablecloths and colorful flower arrangements. There was a long table with serving dishes of savory scented food. Waiters were scurrying out with baskets of rolls and water pitchers for the tables. People were meandering in to select a seat next to friends.

Dinner was lovely but the typical menu. Chicken, ham, rice, green beans, and salad. The Minneapolis studio table was silent even when dessert was served – a strawberry parfait topped with whipped cream and a whole berry. Edward sat at the front table with the other owners. Ashley Dobbs didn't attend dinner.

When the meal was over, the waiters cleaned up the plates, and Paddy set up the music system for the dance. Edward Garrett stood up and spoke into the microphone. He welcomed the other studios and announced he and his partner would provide the entertainment for the evening with a Mambo. He took off his jacket and hung it on the back of his chair, loosened his tie and motioned for the music to begin. Then with a flourish he took the floor and suddenly the double doors flew opened. Ashley Dobbs strutted out to the floor in a sequined Latin dance skirt and short cropped top. The edge of the skirt flipped as she swiveled to the floor. Her hair was wound around her head with glitter spray shimmering in the overhead spot light. She shimmied and shook to the music while Edward circled. They faced each other and began to dance, pulsing to the Latin beat. Ashley's quick feet displayed tight crisp footwork, and her lithe limbs were model smooth as they shaped with opened confidence. The crowd stood up and cheered as they finished their number. Edward rolled Ashley out to the side to take her bow. She smiled and with enthusiasm blinked toward Edward. The two of them pranced off the floor and hand in hand passed through the double doors.

"They were good!" Sydney gushed. Megan and Carson nodded. "Very good."

VI.

The weekend was a success. A huge success. But the week after was a mess. In fact the whole studio fell apart.

KC's weekend report should have been a sign. Amanda Garrett appeared at the front door of the studio early on Monday morning dressed in a sleek black silk blouse softly ruffled around her shoulders and elongated neckline, slim black pants trimmed with a metallic belt, and patent black pumps with three inch killer heels. Her normal casual workout attire was replaced with not only this stunning outfit but a stylish shoulder length hair curled in a frame around her narrow face and make-up that was fashion show perfect even down to the false eyelashes giving her a Bambi eyed look. Her lips pressed tightly together and without saying a word, she motioned with her head toward Edward's closed office door. Megan Meeker sitting at the desk completing the weekly studio reports glanced up giving Amanda a quick nod. "Are you home early? We weren't expecting you until …". Megan's voice trailed off as Amanda didn't bother to knock on the door but instead barged in and slammed the door behind her. "Oh, my." Megan let her hands cover her mouth.

Almost instantly the arguing began. Edward Garrett's voice was not a part of the exploding sound. No, Amanda's voice was elevated to levels Megan had never heard before. Sweet Amanda was like a screaming banshee. Luckily Megan was the only other person in the studio on this early morning after a dance event. She thought about getting up and putting on some loud background music to drown out the sound but instead sat quietly still – listening. What she understood from the bits and pieces that waifed out to the reception area was a horrible disturbing case of infidelity that was not only a shocking heartbreak for a newlywed, but a total breakdown of trust in someone else close to her heart – Ashley Dobbs. Amanda had decided to make a quick surprise trip home and found the two in bed together. Two of her favorite and most trusted people had broken her heart and destroyed her faith in people. Amanda's voice was angry and raging yet pitifully sad and distraught. The half hour rant fluctuated from screeches to sobs. All ranges of emotion poured from behind the closed door, and when it was over Amanda Garrett practically sprinted from the office and back out the front door of the studio leaving Edward Garrett slumped at his desk with his head buried in his outstretched hands.

Meekly his strained voice called out to Megan. "Miss Meeker…". She swiftly appeared in his doorway leaning on the door frame for support.

"Yes?" She was surprised he even remembered she was in the studio. What could he want of her?

"Could you get my friend Oscar Rehm from the New Orleans studio on the phone, please?" His voice was thin and weak. He didn't bother to look up nor did he close his door as he conversed with his friend.

"Oscar? I have a favor to ask of you. Could you use a new female teacher? She's young and quite well trained in the dancing. Needs some work in the teaching area, but should be an asset to your school." He listened politely for a few minutes adding a few "ah has" and "hums" to the conversation that was now dominated from the other end of the phone. Evidently Edward was pawning off his new prodigy on a friend in an attempt to sooth the raging Amanda Garrett. He had made a choice, and it was not going to be the young Ashley Dobbs for him.

For the next week, the other teachers in the studio tiptoed around as if they would be next. It all happened so quickly. Most did not know the details of the whole situation. There were rumors and stories and guesses as to all that happened. But the only truth everyone knew for sure, Ashley Dobbs was gone. Megan Meeker quietly kept Amanda and Edward's conversation a secret. No need for everyone to know all the gory details.

Then the week continued. Déjà vu. Laura Dobbs showed up in a fury. She didn't wait for an announcement of her presence. Instead she let herself into Edward's office and managed to break a few pieces of Caribbean artifacts in the process. She screamed all the way out of the office pointing her finger and tossing whatever was in her way to the floor. Megan cowered behind the reception desk hoping the front window wouldn't shatter when Laura Dobbs threw a vase that careened off the door frame. She certainly didn't appear to be near death on this occasion. Far from it. She was a fierce, snarling jungle cat poised and ready for the attack.

But that wasn't the end of Edward's week of hell. On Friday, a messenger arrived with his divorce papers. Was that all there was to Edward and Amanda's marriage? Oh no. Certainly not. Amanda continued to come in each morning for exercise class, and after a few weeks of Edward pouting and feeling sorry for himself as a partnerless dancer, she agreed to become his temporary partner until a new one could be found. They ranted and raved as usual, but also could be heard laughing and joking during their rehearsal times. Was this a good sign? Could there be a reconciliation in the near future?

Things seemed to be heading in a more positive direction until the next fateful day. It was the day Edward received an early morning call during rehearsal. Megan was once again in working on paperwork and happened to answer the phone. She growled a crisp "Dance studio" into the phone at the interruption. Her eyes drooped from the strains of the past week and her patience was worn thin.

"Mr. Garrett?" she poked her head around the corner of the reception desk. "You have a phone call."

Edward's face turned toward her in a sour grimace. "Never, never, never interrupt me during morning rehearsals!" he screamed. "Take a message!"

Megan hissed inside but continued persistently. "I think you need to take this one …". Megan sighed but remained solid. She had made a judgment call and was not going to back down. She held out the phone and pursed her lips to let him know she meant business.

He reluctantly got up from his stretching position on the floor and taking the space in only two long strides, snatched the phone from her hand and almost yelling, panted into the phone, "This is Edward Garrett. What do you want?"

Suddenly his demeanor softened. He leaned up against the desk and silently listened slowly shrinking from his former tall upright posture. His hostility melted within seconds. Without so much as a reply, he replaced the phone in the cradle and stood in stunned silence.

"What is wrong with you?" Amanda Garrett had gotten to her feet and padded out to the reception area to see what could be so disturbing. Her bare feet wrapped slightly in torn pale tights that she personally had cut the toes and heels off with a dull scissors she had snatched earlier from the front desk. She was back to her casual self – cut up tights with holes and a drooping leotard draped with a faded sweatshirt. After all, what was the point of dressing up for Edward? She certainly didn't need to impress him. He was already eager as a tail wagging puppy to impress her any way he could.

"Ashley tried to commit suicide," he whispered. "They have her in the hospital right now and will transfer her to the psych ward when she is physically better."

Edward couldn't allow his eyes to meet Amanda's. And in turn, her eyes searching his face could not make eye contact with him either. Her lips rounded into an "Oh". They both sighed and slouched in despair.

"Does Laura know about this?" Amanda finally managed to speak.

"That was Oscar, and no, she does not. Oscar thought it best if the doctors call her instead of you or me. I must agree. The news coming from us would make a bad situation even worse," he spoke quietly.

Amanda nodded. She turned and grabbed her duffle bag stuffing it with some of the clothes she had shed during class. Rehearsal was over. And when Edward left to change his clothes, he didn't return – not for three days. The mood in the studio during those days was one of confusion, gossip, and concern. Even those who were not particularly close to the young Ashley, showed a heartfelt worry for her condition both physically and mentally. She was clearly in a state of distress. A state she could not handle.

VII.

Concern for Ashley's situation was soon replaced with plans for the annual upcoming wedding show. Minneapolis was home to one of the nation's largest fashion stores – Daltons. A family owned store, it looked and felt like money and style. Each year Daltons sponsored a wedding fashion show at Orchestra Hall – a stunning building that housed the many musical concerts common in the city. Edward Garrett had landed the coveted choreography spot for the event, much to Amanda's dismay. Now that Amanda was back in Minneapolis, she was trying her hand at choreographing fashion shows. With her incredible background as a top model and her experience in dance, she was a perfect choice. However, in this case, the committee had chosen Edward over Amanda. She was not happy although she graciously supported Edward with the project. That was Amanda's way of course. The event was enormous with a sure turnout of many hundreds of brides and their wedding parties. There would be not only the models in their stunning wedding gowns, but walkways packed with every wedding associated business possible. There would be florists, wedding planners, photographers, caterers, bakers, musicians, hair stylists, manicurists, calligraphers, and of course dance studios. It would be an incredible event. A must attend for any soon-to-be bride.

Edward would have the studio staff performing a few dance numbers, but he wasn't concerned with the dancing as he normally would have been. He would let

Carson try his hand at choreography in the dance demonstrations. Edward was more concerned with the models and how they would prance out on the runway. So he plunged right in to design a fashion show presentation. He was determined to show ex-wife Amanda that he was capable of presenting a fabulous fashion show. His demeanor was one of a new grittiness and spunk. He had new purpose.

Carson carefully put together a short Waltz routine that would include himself, Paddy, and Jim as the males dancing with Sydney, Claire and Mary. Then they would dance a swing to a popular country song about a bride wearing blue jeans. The women would be fitted for wedding gowns for the Waltz, and then he and Claire would do the swing wearing jeans on a ramp sloped over the audience heads as the other two couples would remain in their gowns and tuxes performing on the center stage. He loved the idea as did Edward.

Sydney felt like a blimp compared to the tiny and young Claire and Mary, but she graciously slipped into the dress the Dalton's staff had chosen she wear. It looked lovely. It had capped lace sleeves and a sweetheart neckline with a fitted bodice and ball gown-like skirt that gently surfed the floor as she walked. "This will dance well," she announced twirling. With a shrug of her shoulders, she retreated to the changing room to don her street clothes.

Claire was zipped into another traditional gown with a fitted bodice, drop waistline and full skirt. Her sheer

61

top was close fitting with a scalloped neckline. Mary was originally placed into a mermaid style dress fitting tightly down her hips and legs to a floating tail-like skirt at the bottom, but Sydney quickly explained it would not be appropriate to dance a Waltz. Mary would not be able to stretch her legs as she tried to twinkle – a common Waltz step - across the stage. They decided instead on a dress with a fuller skirt but an a-line silhouette that looked sleek on her tiny frame.

The show would be on a Saturday – a day the studio was normally closed to regular lessons. Sydney usually scheduled a few Saturday lessons and would move them to times during the week to do the show. It would be worthwhile – even if she had to wear a wedding gown.

Megan Meeker enthusiastically accepted the position as booth attendant. She really enjoyed this event and knew how much business the crowds could bring in to the studio. On this day of the event, she gathered together a large carrying case filled with brochures, business cards and photos of other wedding couples as they danced to the music during their special day. She picked through the stack of pictures and selected the best ones showing couples looking especially elegant. Megan knew it was important to look businesslike yet classy in order to entice the young women and their mothers to stop at her booth. Should she play music? She looked at herself in the mirror and grinned. Her canary yellow suit buttoned down the front with a flattering full skirt, wide yellow and black belt cinching in her tiny waist, and a gathered capped sleeve.

To match, she had on a pair of yellow pointy toed pumps and a wide brimmed yellow hat with a black band holding in a few strategically placed fake daisies. Perfect!

It was quite easy to walk down the street to the block long Orchestra Hall building with its peaked contemporary shaped glass eaves. It was Saturday, and the dancers would meet in their dressing room to dress for the show. Megan would set up the dance booth in the venders hallway and maybe get a quick glance at their performance when the main fashion show began. It was the main event and would pull most of the attendees into the auditorium for a look at the latest fashions this season for both bride and bridesmaid. She was sure the hallways would be almost empty. She hoped her booth was positioned near an auditorium entrance so she could scamper over for a peek.

Sydney Monroe paced back and forth in the tiny dressing room assigned to the dancers just behind the stage entrance. There were the three wedding gowns hanging from the hooks looking like spun sugar – lacy and fluffy. She had unpacked her dress and waited to slip into it just before the routine was to start. Jim and Paddy were outside the door. She could tell because Paddy's voice was booming. Carson was already dressed in his tux as were the other two men – traditional black with black cummerbunds, pleated white shirts and black bow ties. Their dance shoes easily finished the look. So where were the other two ladies? Not to worry yet. They still had time. Sydney began to rub her hands together and take in deep breaths of air. She was always early and had rituals to take up time. Closing her eyes, she began to meditate, mentally moving over each step in the routines.

Meanwhile, finding her booth, Megan placed the brochures and cards on the table then carefully displayed the photos placing a few on easels for a better view. Nothing like a photo to create an image. She saw Amanda Garrett scurry down the hall toward the changing rooms. Amanda was dressed all in black which seemed to be her favorite color since the breakup of her marriage. Megan wondered if it was a statement about her mood rather than the style of the outfit. Where was Edward? Probably lining up his models. She could imagine he was probably in his usual state of nervous energy - that is if he was even here. She hoped he wouldn't be late as usual today of all days. Not today!

The crowds were getting heavier. Giddy young women dragged along friends and family to look over all the services provided. Many stopped to pickup cards and even ask about scheduling appointment times for lessons. People smiled and pointed at the photos before moving on to the cake maker booth next in line. The cakes on display were amazingly delicious looking. Megan wanted badly to look through their cake books. It didn't matter if she wasn't going to be a bride in the near future. Those cakes looked very inviting. Occasionally Megan would catch a glimpse of someone she thought she knew – a student, former student or just a familiar face. There were just so many people milling around waiting for the show to begin.

Back in the dressing room, Sydney pulled on her dress and opened the door. Mary scurried in frantically pawing at the plastic covering her dress. "Where is Claire?" Sydney hissed.

"What? Isn't she here yet?" Mary frowned looking around the room with a new frightened look in her eyes. "I thought she would already be here. We were suppose to meet at the corner and come over together. But she never showed! I thought she must have forgotten and went in alone. Let me call her,"

Mary pulled out her phone and punched in the numbers. After a few seconds, she pulled the phone away from her ear and flipped it closed. "No answer," she shook her head. "I can't imagine where she could be. This is not like Claire at all!"

"Well, we have to go on soon. So we better have a backup plan in case she doesn't show," Sydney began with panic in her voice nibbling nervously on her already short fingernails. "What can we do?"

Sydney slipped out the door and found Carson pacing in the hallway. "Claire is a no show!" she announced. "What will we do now?"

Carson looked around pressing down the hairs on his dark mustache. "The routines are clearly choreographed for three couples. It's too late to redo the routines. We only have one choice, I think. We'll have to

65

enlist Megan. She's sitting in the studio booth. I'll go get her right now."

Moments later, Carson returned dragging – literally – Megan Meeker in her canary yellow dress and hat. "You want me to what???" she bantered back and forth with Carson. Paddy snickered in the corner as Megan placed her feet solidly on the floor with her hands on her ample hips and demanded to know what exactly she was expected to do.

Carson explained Claire had not yet showed up. Megan would have to slip into Claire's wedding dress and do the Waltz. He would lead her through the routine although they were the first in line to enter the stage. "It's an easy basic Waltz, Megan," he pleaded. "You'll have no problem doing the routine. Then we do a swing. That one is a bit more complicated..." he started to ponder for a moment. "Sydney, you'll have to do the solo with me in the jeans, and Megan can dance with Paddy in the wedding dress, I guess."

At this both women seemed to panic. Megan threw up her hands. "Can't you just have two couples dancing? I'm not worried about the Waltz routine – it's fitting into the wedding dress that scares me. Do you actually think I can wear little tiny Claire's dress? I don't think so!" The tone in her voice rose an octave.

Sydney also shook her head violently with a concerned look on her face as well. "You know I'm not good with heights, Carson. Me on that ramp? I don't know about that."

Carson turned to both women and simply announced, "We have no choice. Daltons wants all three dresses displayed. We are part of the fashion show. We need three couples to dance. That's what we are going to have to do to get through this event. So stop arguing and get dressed." Quiet Carson was taking charge. He rubbed his forehead with his fingers trying to massage out the beginning of a possible splitting headache his forehead furrowing into a deep crevice. The women were silenced and feeling guilty they had pushed him to this point with their whining complaints.

Sydney and Megan disappeared inside the dressing room and began to make adjustments. Clearly Claire's dress would not fit Megan although she had a tiny waist. She also had wide hips and voluptuous breasts. So Megan slipped instead into Sydney's dress, and Sydney took Claire's. They were both too large for the dress Claire was to wear, but Sydney might make the transition a little easier. Megan couldn't completely zip up the white dress she was wearing, so Sydney folded back the top of the back and pinned the zipper so it wouldn't slide down during the routines. All they needed was the dress to split or unzip during the show! Talk about compounding disaster upon disaster.

Sydney handed Megan an extra pair of dance shoes she happened to carry in her dance bag. Megan certainly couldn't wear those pointy toed yellow pumps with the white wedding dress. Megan groaned but managed to cinch the Latin sandals on with ease. They were silver but would have to do. Who would see them beneath the voluminous fabric of her dress anyway?

"I personally feel like a stuffed sausage," Sydney announced as she viewed the dress she wore with skepticism. She couldn't help but notice the way the white satin fabric rolled around her waistline in unbecoming lumps. "Let's just get through this as quickly and simply as we can." The two nodded in agreement as Mary sat in the corner with a deeply worried look on her face. Where was her friend? This was so unlike Claire.

"Let's do this, boys!" Megan shouted enthusiastically as they lined up along the back of the stage. She did a quick round of high fives to all in the hallway. Carson and Megan were first with Paddy and Sydney behind and Mary with Jim in the rear. The stage was dark. Multiple rows of curtains hung darkly on all sides in looming shadows. It felt like a forest of fabric. Carson explained they would do Waltz runs out to the floor and when they reached the center, the spot light would suddenly light up, and the show would begin. The Waltz was the opening act followed by a line- up of models, and then half way through the show their Swing routine would begin the second portion.

"Just follow me and don't worry!" Carson hissed in Megan's ear as they waited for their introduction.

Carson put Megan on his right side in a shadow position and led her out to the floor. Unfortunately, the stage crew in an attempt to cool down the stage ahead of time had placed several portable air conditioners on the stage floor. After they had turned them off just before the event was to begin, the oily condensed water from these units had leaked a wide streak of liquid across the floor. Carson and Megan of course in the dark didn't see the glistening line on the stage. As they started out toward the center, the lights flashed just as Megan stepped on the oil and began to slip uncontrollably across the floor with Carson frantically trying to follow her sliding right over the slick stage. Megan began to scream, "Shiiiiii...t" just as Carson snatched her under her armpits before she could land in the front row of spectators who gazed up in agonizing horror. Their mouths gaped open and a loud gasp could be heard above the swaying flow of the Waltz music turned up to high capacity in the background. Paddy and Sydney who followed luckily spotted the slick oil before they reached the spot in the floor and successfully avoided the area as did Jim and Mary. The rest of the routine went smoothly although by now, the crowd was in a startled titter. Megan was not smiling – she wore a tight mouthed grimace across her face. Luckily it was a short routine, and the models began to weave across the floor immediately after the dancers' exit in long lines of fashionable elegance, and the crowds were replacing their laughter with "Oohs" and "Aahs".

Sydney scrambled out of her wedding dress and pulled on her jeans grumbling with each tug. Grabbing the long lacy veil she was to wear for the Swing, she attached it with hair pins to the top of her dark banged hairdo. "Oh, my", she sighed looking briefly into the mirror hanging at a bit of a tilt on the changing room wall.

"What's the matter? I already stole the show. What more can happen?" Megan moaned as she slumped in the chair in the corner flattening the back of her poufy wedding skirt. "I've never been so embarrassed in my whole life. Wait until I get a hold of Claire!" she grunted.

"I'm scared to death of heights," explained Sydney. "I don't know what will happen if I try to dance up there on that ramp up over everyone's heads. Is Carson strong enough to hold on to me?" Sydney looked skeptical.

"Well he snagged me, didn't he? He is a hero as far as I'm concerned otherwise I'd be sprawled out in the middle of that crowd with a puffy white skirt wrapped unceremoniously around my head." Megan decided to remember to thank him for his courageous rescue.

The Swing routine was just as much a disaster as far as Carson was concerned. Paddy and Megan, Jim and Mary danced down on the stage in tuxes and wedding gowns hopefully drawing most of the attention of the spectators. Carson and Sydney managed to climb up the ramp to the middle of the narrow space above the heads of the audience at first bringing all eyes up, but when Carson started to lead the routine, Sydney froze and refused to do anything that involved a turn of any kind. She clung to him in a state of panic with her veil trailing over the edge of the

70

ramp leaving him helpless to lead the choreographed routine. He finally sighed and just did a few basic steps before guiding Sydney down off the structure as the audience craned their necks to see them hanging above their heads. Then they sprinted off the stage. Sydney remained in a state of panic for several minutes as she sprawled out on the floor of the dressing room. Mary tried to hang and pack up the dresses, struggling with the awkward fullness of the skirts and the narrow plastic bags they were to somehow fit in.

Megan had scurried off to man her booth again. She watched as the attendees filed out of the auditorium after the show ended. In the back of her mind, she prayed the wide brimmed yellow hat hid her face and no one would recognize her as the foul mouthed dancer who had careened across the stage floor and almost into the audience. She gazed around and thought she spotted another familiar face. A tall dark haired beauty and her mother stopped at the table. Megan pointed and asked, "Annie?" The smiling young woman smiled and introduced herself. "Annie St. Germaine." She held out her hand. Megan returned the polite hand shake.

"Are you planning a wedding?" Megan grinned and looked from face to face. The two seemed to freeze in their expressions, then Annie calmly said, "Yes, in the distant future though." Her smile was wooden and fixed.

"What a lucky man to have you as a wife," Megan nodded. Then she was distracted by another soon-to-be bride asking a question about the brochure and when she looked back, Annie St. Germaine was gone.

Still struggling with the dresses and the bags, Mary began to frantically look around. "Oh, my." Mary shook her head as she finished putting the plastic covering over the long white dresses. "One of my drop pearl earrings is missing." She was fingering one of her earlobes. Everyone except Megan of course, had put on jewelry provided by Daltons to match their dresses. Mary had worn a pair of earrings in a large white pearl teardrop shape. "How can you lose something this big?" she threw up her hands in dismay. "It's probably worth a fortune as well."

"I'll help you find it," Sydney had gotten to her feet and was not shaking as badly as she had a few minutes earlier. Still in her jeans, she flung the lacy veil over the bagged dresses. "I'm sure it has to be here, in the hall or on the stage. "

They scoured the small dressing room, but found nothing. So they spread out along the small hallway that led to the stage and followed the path to the almost dark curtained area. Lights were on in the auditorium as workers were cleaning up the aisles of seats for programs and other paper debris. Mary took one side of the stage, and Sydney took the other. Sydney got down on her knees and felt along under the heavy curtains that seemed to be everywhere. There appeared to be something shiny under the fabric, and she tried to push it back for a better look. Finally, she tried to go back behind the curtain for a different angle. That's when she pulled back the curtain –

there hanging in the fabric folds was a body held up by a stage cord around the neck. It was Edward Garrett. His feet were grazing the floor as his body has held by the cord wrapped tightly under his chin. His head was lilting to the left with his toupee slightly slipping down over his forehead. Sydney shuddered and called hoarsely for Mary. The two of them held each other at the sight, and then called out loudly for the workers in the auditorium to call the police. Sydney was once again shaking. It had been a very bad day.

Megan Meeker heard the rumbling from the workers as they scurried out whispering and shaking their heads. After she packed everything up into two cardboard boxes, she spotted the uniformed men heading to the auditorium and decided to find out what was happening. Peeking in around the heavy door, she spotted Sydney, Mary and now Carson and Paddy up on the stage in animated discussion with one of the policemen. Carson was using his hands in a most agitated manner. She hurried up the aisle and joined the group as they gazed on the still hanging body.

"Oh, my! Oh, my!" she gasped and felt herself get weak in the knees. Carson once again caught her under her arm pits and held her up. She rested her head on his shoulder as he lowered her gently to the ground. "Oh, my," sighed Megan. "Amanda! Has anyone found Amanda?"

The policeman looked confused. "Edward Garrett's wife. Oh, ex-wife," Sydney Monroe explained with a nod. She looked back at Megan still sitting on the floor. "Is

Amanda here? Why? Why would she be here? Is she modeling?"

Megan shook her head gently. "I don't know why she is here, but I saw her come in and go back stage earlier today before the show began."

"And when was this?" the policeman looked interested as he stood poised with his notepad. His dark uniform was crisp and neat on his looming figure – he was a tall, large boned man with a young but beefy face. His hair was slicked back against his head and was beginning to thin at the temples. Of course he would be interested in an ex-wife. A dead body and an ex-wife? Quite a tempting combination. Almost a sure bet for closing his case immediately.

"She ran down the hallway at the beginning of the event way before the show began. I know she helps Edward sometimes with choreography, but it seemed odd to see her here today for some reason. She was a bit upset that Edward got the choreography job over her. She would have been a more obvious choice with her background as a model and all." The policeman raised an eyebrow.

Carson motioned to the policeman that he would go backstage and look to see if she was still here, and the officer nodded his approval as he continued to interview the women who found the body. Carson raced off down the hallway to find the area the models used for changing rooms. Would they still be there? Yes, as he approached the rooms he spotted a model sauntering out of one room

74

carrying a large duffle bag. She was tall and thin with a hunched over stoop in her posture.

"Excuse me," Carson called out with a wave of his hand as he began to run down the hall. "Is Amanda Garrett here?"

The model looked over her shoulder, a long blond bang falling over her eyes now rimmed with pooling black mascara. She nodded and flicked her head back toward the room she had just exited. "She's in there." Her voice was raspy and soft. She shifted her bag back up on her shoulder and with leggy strides strutted down the hallway toward the exit sign.

Carson rapped on the door before entering. Amanda Garrett, dressed in her black pants and black shell top turned to see who was entering the room. She frowned when she saw Carson – not because she disliked the man, but simply because he was a man. She was like a mother hen with her very young models, and a man dropping in on their dressing rooms was not something she tolerated. She was gathering the dresses and putting plastic bags on each one.

"We need you right away on the stage," Carson announced in a quick but sharp tone. Should he tell her why? Should he be the one? This was certainly a task he dreaded.

Amanda frowned. "I'm not even supposed to be here," she announced angrily. "Edward never showed up for the show and one of the models called me just before walk on was about to begin. Someone needed to line up the girls and get the show on track. I know Edward sometimes is late for appointments, but this is unacceptable. And very unlike Edward to just never show up! Especially for something so very important to him and his career." She was clearly frustrated as she flung a plastic bag onto the floor. "What's on the stage? Isn't it something someone else can handle? I'm terribly busy getting all of these gowns packed up." Her hand pulled on one of the skirts smoothing out a wrinkle at the hemline.

"Amanda," Carson said softly gazing into her eyes. She blinked trying not to meet his gaze. It was as if she knew already. Carson walked across the room and gripped her hand. "Edward didn't show up because he is dead." She pulled her hand away and put her hands over her face. Carson continued. "Edward's body is on the stage. He's been murdered."

"What?" Amanda's face twisted in disbelief. "I knew something had to be wrong – when Edward didn't show up for the show, I knew something wasn't right. But murdered? Dead? How can that be?"

Carson put his arms around her shoulders trying to comfort her, then he gently led her out the door and toward the stage. Amanda introduced herself to the policeman still in conversation with Sydney, Megan, Mary, and Paddy. Two other uniformed men were trying to lower the body of Edward Garrett from the rope. Amanda glanced at the effort and then tried to avert her eyes from the slump of the man she had been married to and loved. She bit her lower lip in anguish. Her stomach ached at the sight.

When the body had been carried off the stage, the officer asked if he could speak privately with Amanda, and they moved down to the front row of seats – the same ones Megan had almost landed in earlier that day. Carson shared the information Amanda had told him about Edward's absence at the show. Megan and Sydney nodded their heads at the news, but Mary began to wring her hands frantically. "Where could Claire be?" she brought the conversation back to another concern. Edward Garrett hadn't shown up for the show, and he was now dead. Where could Claire be? What was her fate?

Megan motioned to the officer, interrupting his conversation with Amanda Garrett. "I don't mean to interrupt, but we are also missing one of our dancers who was supposed to be in the show. We're concerned about her as well." She told him about Claire.

"Was she involved with Mr. Edward Garrett in any way?" the officer asked with a frown.

"Personally? No. She was his employee, but that was all. At least I think that's all it was." Now it was Megan's turn to frown. Had she paid attention to the interaction in the studio enough to know what she was saying was true? Yes. She believed it was true. Then where was Claire? Behind her Mary was now in tears. Carson was again the one to hold her up. What a day! Carson Hunter was not a man of great emotion or affection

77

– well liked but not particularly teary eyed or gushy. Yet, today Carson Hunter was the shoulder everyone seemed to lean on. He was the hero of the day. The rock. Now he was comforting a wailing Mary with gentle compassion.

Megan began to wring her hands as her mind churned in thought. What could they tell the officer about Claire? She let her mind flash back to her booth in the wedding show hallway. Had she noticed a photo of any kind in her display of Claire? Yes, she thought so. She felt energized. At least for that brief moment. Racing down the aisle to the now empty table that once was a colorful display, she began to paw through the box she had just packed. There was a stack of photos she had used in the display. She grabbed the pile and returned to the auditorium trying to glance at the pictures as she walked back to the stage. She handed half of the stack to Carson and asked him to look through to see if there was a photo of Claire in any of the pictures. They both scoured the party scenes looking for the girl's face.

"Got one," Carson announced shoving a glossy print under Megan's nose. Yes, there it was. Mary and Claire were posing for the camera. They had their arms around each other with Paddy and Jim behind them. A group photo, but it would give the officer a good idea of the young woman's appearance. Claire was smiling, her light brown straight hair flowing behind her. They passed along the photo to the officer who was now finishing up with Amanda and would want to question Mary more about her dear friend.

"I hope you realize there are three possibilities here with Claire's disappearance," Megan was whispering to Carson. She continued, "One, she murdered Edward Garrett. Two, she saw who murdered Edward Garrett. And three, something totally unrelated to Edward Garrett caused her to miss this show. Like a car accident or something else equally horrible."

Carson nodded. He moved toward the officer and asked in a low voice so as not to disturb Mary, "Do you think you could find out if anyone answering Claire's description could have had an accident of any kind? You know, been admitted to the hospital or something like that?"

The officer pulled out his phone attached to his belt and nodding called the station for any news on a young woman that could have been reported that morning. Then he asked if they could put some calls into local hospitals. He gazed at the photo and tried to relate as best he could what she looked like for the person on the other end of the phone. "Her name is Claire..," looking around for Carson, he waited to complete his sentence. Carson mouthed "Claire Benson". "Benson. Her name is Claire Benson," the officer finished his thought.

Carson put his arm around Mary and then gently pulled up a folding chair from the back corner for the officer to interview her about anything she knew about Claire. Mary seemed to be the best source of information about the woman. Carson had to admit he knew very little.

Mary explained through sobs, "Claire lived in a small one bedroom apartment in Dinkytown. She just graduated from the U so just kept her housing as she tried to find a job. She didn't have a car, but would meet me at the studio every day after working a few hours at her part-time job. It was just a few hours at one of the small stores by the campus. I live in the uptown area, so we were really in opposite directions. We were supposed to meet this morning at quarter to nine in front of Orchestra Hall so we could get dressed for the show. But she never came. I assumed she got there early and just went in to find the changing room." Then after a few more wails, she continued. "She never showed up there either!"

"So she lives alone?" the officer asked trying to be calming. Mary nodded. Silence. "Where does she work part-time?" Mary mentioned a well-known shop along University Avenue but added, "She wasn't scheduled to work today because of the show and all." The officer nodded.

"Does she have any family or close friends nearby?" He sat poised with his pen ready to write.

"Just me. That's all I know of. Her family lives down in southern Minnesota, and we became best friends when we started at the studio. Her college friends had already moved away after graduation. So I haven't met anyone else she would have been close to," Mary's red rimmed eyes blinked uncontrollably.

"No boyfriend?" he ventured another possibility.

"No. No one special at the moment," Mary seemed to be thinking back to anything that could be of help.

"No enemies?" he continued.

"Oh, no. Claire was friends with everyone. Everyone loved her!" This sent Mary into another crying binge.

"Do you have her phone number?" he asked hoping this might stop the tears.

"Yes. Oh, yes. But she didn't answer when I called her this morning. Did she, Sydney?" She looked around to find Sydney Monroe who was standing in the group behind her chair. Sydney managed to shake her head. "Can you try again?" Mary gave the number to the officer who again dialed the number only to come up with a voice message.

As the group was beginning to break up, Megan Meeker cornered the officer with some questions of her own. "Do you think whoever did this," she began, "had to have a great deal of strength to hang Edward up like that?"

"Actually," he looked at her with a slightly pondering look. Should he give her the information he had? "From our preliminary findings, it appears Mr. Garrett was struck on the head rendering him unconscious before the rope was tied around his neck. Then with the way these curtains are on pulleys, someone with very little effort could have hung him. Strength wouldn't have been a factor here."

Megan nodded with a grimace on her face. "Will you let us know if you find Claire?"

He smiled and nodded taking down her personal phone number as well as the address and phone number for the studio. "Are you a good contact person?" he asked.

"I'm the manager of the studio. Yes, I'm a good contact person," she nodded wondering what would become of the studio and her job now that Edward was deceased. Another thing to think about. She sighed. This had been a very difficult day.

Megan suddenly grabbed Carson as they walked out of the building. "I think we need to look around, Carson."

"What do you mean?" he looked particularly tired.

"I have a terrible feeling about sweet little Claire, and I think we should look around the neighborhood a bit before we head home." Both of them lived relatively close together and frequently took the same bus home. "I am concerned."

The two of them began circling the mammoth building and looked in the corners and areas partially covered by landscaping and bushes but to no avail. Nothing seemed out of the ordinary. They moved up and down the block checking backs of buildings as they circled. "Let's check the bus schedules," Megan suggested with a flash of an idea. "Let's see when Claire's bus would have arrived this morning."

The downtown area was blocked off from regular traffic except for the buses – lots and lots of buses. There were enclosed bus shelters on each block going in both directions with bus schedules plastered up on the walls for riders to check destinations and times. They found the shelter right across from the Hall and looked up and down for the bus that would have come from Dinkytown. Checking the routes, they zeroed in on one that looked promising. Sliding their fingers down the times for Saturday, they found a few that might have been perfect for Claire to take downtown this morning.

"Look at this one," Megan motioned. "If Claire had taken this one, she would have gotten here about a half hour earlier than Mary. What would she do? Get a coffee. Maybe."

Megan dug into her pocket where she still had the photo she showed the officer. "Let's check around." Orchestra Hall was a few blocks up the street from the studio. So normally, Claire wouldn't have frequented any of the coffee shops in this block. She could have been a regular down closer to the studio block, but not in this area. If anyone recognized her, it would most likely been from a visit today. No harm in trying. Saturdays in the downtown area were not very crowded or busy except in the evenings when the nightlife began. So they might have luck finding someone who had spotted and remembered Claire this morning. Most businesses were closed on Saturdays, so traffic was relatively slow. They began at one small shop and received a negative response, but the second one was different. It was close to the corner where Claire would have gotten off the bus. Yes, one worker remembered her. She had purchased a black coffee and a small muffin. They had chatted a bit because there was no one else around at that time. She had mentioned she was going to the wedding show at Orchestra Hall.

"What time would that have been?" Megan eagerly asked.

"Maybe around 8:20. It wasn't yet 8:30 because that's when my other worker was scheduled to arrive, and she wasn't here yet," the clerk pondered just how the schedule must have worked.

"Thanks!" Megan looked around for a business card and frantically copied down the clerk's name on the card. It was clearly printed on her nametag – "Jennifer".

As they left the shop, Megan put in a call to the police officer to report their new find. "I think you should search Orchestra Hall again," Megan suggested. "I think something happened to Claire Benson, and it is important we find her fast. She may be in danger or worse. She could be dead as well. The workers probably have picked up anything of value and tossed it already during their cleaning."

Megan seemed frustrated by the response she received on the other end of the phone, but she finally hung up and turned to face the now exhausted Carson who was seated on the bus bench hoping they could take the next bus home. Not to be however.

"The officer is sending a few men to search the Hall, and we are going to help them," she announced stubbornly. Carson slid down lower in his seat. His tongue stuck out and his eyelids closed wearily. "I'll get you a cup of coffee from that nice little shop, and you'll feel good as new!" Megan flounced down to the shop they had just left and ordered two coffees – black. When she arrived back at the bench Carson was now occupying, the other officers arrived and were on their way toward the front entrance. Megan dragged Carson from his seat and they sprinted off to join them for the search. Megan was not in the mood to take "no" from them, and they could sense that in her approach. They said nothing as the two joined the officers as they entered the door met by the cleaning crew to go over the building room by room and area by area. It would take time unless they quickly found something.

Nothing. Nothing of importance was found even though they searched through the rooms, nooks and crannies as well as the bags of garbage already collected. It was a grueling afternoon.

Megan and Carson stepped out into the fresh air and were met with a pleasing aroma. Food! Across from the hall were several pubs with outdoor seating areas. The dinner and evening crowds were beginning to sit at tables to gaze at the beautiful sky and drink imported dark beer.

"Looks good," Carson licked his lips. "I could go for a cold one and a nice hot sandwich. How about you?"

Megan grinned and slid her arm into his. "I'm with you!"

They found a seat across from the hall and leaned back in their chairs sipping beer from frosty glasses waiting for the waiter to deliver their meals. Megan gazed across the square at the people seated around the fountain and the courtyard that entranced the hall. It was certainly busier than it had been earlier, but the wedding parties were also long gone having scattered before noon when the show ended. She spotted some of the street musicians playing violins and guitars with their cases opened for donations.

"What about those people?" She motioned with her head as she took a mouthful of cold beer. "Do you think any of them would have been around early this morning to notice Claire?"

After finishing their tasty sandwiches made with thick sourdough rolls and piles of roast beef and turkey, they licked up the last of the salty chunky cut fries and headed out to talk to some of the street people serenading the evening crowds.

The first man strumming his guitar was a bit grisly with an unshaved face and bandana wrapped around his scrawny neck. He played a country western song and occasionally tried to croon a few words but said he had only just gotten to this corner when Megan tempted him for an answer with a fist full of dollars held over his opened case. But the next woman, a violin player in a colorful layered skirt and peasant blouse nodded. She had been here this morning early. The shelter she stayed in made them leave at 6:30am each morning, she explained. So she usually got to this corner around quarter to seven and hoped for a few bucks for a coffee or small breakfast. She gazed at the photo of Claire and again nodded. She pointed to the corner near the entrance to the hall. She had been standing over there with another person. She couldn't quite remember what that person looked like however. Was it a man or woman? Didn't know. But she remembered the girl, Claire because she had put a few coins in her case as she walked by with her coffee and muffin in hand along with a fairly large duffle bag over her shoulder.

Hmmm. Megan pondered on the ride home in the bus. Another person. Claire had met another person. Who could that person have been? Edward Garrett? Maybe. They did know that Claire had indeed been at Orchestra Hall and was planning to dance in the wedding show. So she hadn't been in any kind of accident on the way downtown. She had actually made it to the hall. Now what?

VIII.

Carson's stop came up first. He said a hasty good-by and swung out the door of the bus to the street. It was only a few short blocks to the two story older home he shared with several college friends. The houses in this area were all large and charming. They had once housed families when first built, but as the city began to expand, most families had moved out to the suburbs and these houses were now occupied by a more bohemian crowd – younger professionals in their twenties and thirties who enjoyed the quaint bars and restaurants in the thriving uptown area only a few blocks beyond. Carson and his college friends had bought one of these houses when they first graduated from college as an investment and the arrangement seemed to work out quite nicely – at least for the time being. It was white with a large airy porch that wrapped around the front of the house. The peaks in the front hid the dormered attic spaces. The houses on their block were close enough to look out the side window into the window of the house next door. But that didn't seem to concern anyone as their block was a close knit community of people who had developed friendships over the past few years.

As he entered the front door, Carson heard the people in the kitchen. His roommates must be having a dinner party. So typical of a Saturday evening. Yes, the long country style table in the adjoining formal dining room was lined with friends and neighbors enjoying bowls of thick wild rice soup and fresh baked bread. There were bottles of wine uncorked and poured into mismatched glasses and crafty goblets. Everyone greeted Carson with a shout and pulled up a chair for him to join them. Soup? No, he had just eaten. Oh well, maybe just a taste. He spooned a mouthful into tired lips and sighed. Delicious! Carson loved soups, and he loved evenings like this.

Normally quiet and laid back, Carson squirmed anxiously in his chair ready to tell his friends about his day. He related the details of the wedding show, Megan sliding across the floor almost into the front row of viewers, and Sydney clinging for dear life on the ramp above the audience. Carson could tell a story with a flourish of humor when he wanted to. The group laughed heartily at the descriptions he related about the show. Then it was on to the body – Edward Garrett hanging from the curtain cord. The group reeled back in shock as he described the initial horror of seeing a dead body. He told the sad tale of Claire's disappearance and how Megan and he had tried to find any tidbit of information as to where she could be. After a moment of heavy silence, the group began to chatter loudly about what could have happened to her. Questions flew about the woman's habits, her character, and her friends or family. Carson answered as best he could, but he soon realized how little he knew about this person he worked with every day. He shook his head and began to massage his temple. Another glass of wine might make this throbbing subside. It had been a very difficult day. He was growing weary. And worried – more worried than he had been earlier. The questions his friends asked spurned new concerns.

About a mile beyond, Megan Meeker had arrived home to an empty studio apartment. She lived on the second floor of a small brick building – one of a number of brick buildings clustered in the complex. Each building was not tall, but rather quaint fitting in nicely with the neighborhood of older homes. Megan's apartment was a one room with bathroom. She unlocked the door and was met with a blast of warm air. She had no air conditioning, so quickly opened the windows and hit the on button for her fan. She gingerly doffed her yellow wide brimmed hat and placed it on a peg in the wall. One long wall was completely decorated with Megan's hats hung on small pegs. It was an interesting arrangement affectionately called her "art". The colorful hats brought the eye quickly to the wall and a hat tree at the end in the corner. There was a brick fireplace along the other wall and a comfy overstuffed couch facing that with a small end table and a tiny television propped on the desk next to the fireplace. The couch provided double duty folding out into Megan's bed at the end of the day. Beyond the desk was a small kitchenette area with a counter, microwave, refrigerator and stovetop. Megan dropped onto the couch flinging her purse toward the desk. She flipped off her yellow pointy toed shoes and rubbed her aching toes before turning on the television. It would be time for the news, and she wanted to see if Edward's death would be a part of the broadcast. She flicked back and forth between the four local news stations before she heard one announce they would be sharing a story about the Dalton's wedding show. She focused in as best she could on the small screen.

"Oh, my!" she groaned when they opened with a clip of her sliding toward the edge of the stage during the Waltz routine. Then the camera panned to a reporter who talked about the death of a local dance studio owner. Without giving out the name, the reporter gave a few vague details ending with "investigators are looking into the possibility of foul play."

"Foul play," Megan shook her head. "Of course it's foul play. He was murdered, for goodness sake!" She wondered if there would be more information later that evening.

Slipping out of her yellow suit, Megan found a comfortable pair of shorts and a t-shirt. The air was beginning to lighten and feel less stifling. What was she going to do about Claire? It was Saturday night. Nothing more could be done at this time. Maybe in the morning she could go back down to the studio and find Claire's employment application. It was important someone notify her family – if there was a family at all. There should be an emergency number listed on the form. Yes, that would be what she could do. She spent the evening cradling the phone nearby in case a call from the police might come to say they had found Claire or maybe had a suspect in the murder. Something. Anything. The television droned on until the news came on again. No new information seemed to be presented on any of the stations. All were as vague as before. Megan pulled out her couch bed and snuggled in until morning. It had been a very long day and she now found herself exhausted. The cool crisp sheets felt soothing and inviting.

Sundays were not good days for the local buses. Megan stood at her corner for a good half hour before a bus stopped to pick her up and head downtown. There were only a few scattered people in the seats. A dressed up couple probably heading down to the large church located a few blocks east of the studio sat directly in front of Megan. When they reached downtown, Megan hopped off of the bus lightly and headed straight for the parking lot with the studio tucked beneath. Most businesses were closed on Sundays, so the parking lot would be quite empty. She unlocked the front door and gazed around the space. It was a strange feeling that suddenly hit her. No longer would Edward Garrett come strolling across the dance floor to that large corner office. No longer would he pat gently on his toupee as he passed in front of the mirror. No more ranting, raving and temper tantrums. Strangely she felt a feeling of loss – she would miss these little irritations. Yes, it would be very different. What would become of this studio? Could they manage without the dynamic personality of Edward Garrett? Yes, they could. She nodded confidently and sucked in a deep breath of air. Yes, she would make this studio work. She and Carson and Sydney and Paddy and Jim and Mary and KC. They would all make it work.

Megan slid behind the front reception desk and pulled out the drawer with the employee files. Flipping through a number of other applications, she found Claire's toward the back of the file. It was a one page piece of paper that did indeed have an emergency number. She stared briefly at the rest of the page to familiarize herself with what information Claire had provided. Nothing much – address in Dinkytown, phone number and education information which included her graduation date from the University with a degree in Sociology. Interesting.

Dancers came with all sorts of backgrounds. She scrolled down the page and found the name and number of Claire's parents. They didn't have the same last name. Mother must have remarried after a death or divorce. The area code was from southern Minnesota, and Megan dialed the number. She glanced at her watch – clocks were strictly forbidden in the studio. Edward didn't like to be reminded how late he was for meetings or appointments. Yes, it was late enough on a Sunday morning to make a call, she decided. After a few rings, a woman answered.

"Hello, I'm Megan Meeker calling in regards to Claire Benson. Are you Claire's mother?" Megan tried to sound upbeat although her heart was heavy with the news she was about to relate if this was indeed Claire's relative.

"Why, yes," the woman sounded almost eager to continue the conversation.

Megan related the events briefly of the previous day without going into the murder at all – not at this point. She said the studio was concerned about Claire because she hadn't shown up for their show. Had they heard any news from Claire?

The mother's voice began to sound concerned. No, they had been out of contact with Claire for the past year or so. Evidently there was an argument about Claire and her school decisions. The woman had not even known Claire was working at the dance studio. This was surprising news for her. Dancing had never been something Claire seemed particularly interested in growing up.

Megan asked about any friends, but her mother didn't seem to know much about Claire and her life in the cities at all. Her voice sounded weaker and more troubled. It was as if Megan had dredged up something the woman had tried to forget. Megan didn't pry any more, but asked if the family heard anything from Claire could they call the studio and let them know? Certainly. Megan gave her the number and also her personal number in case any news came after studio hours, then she hung up with a sunken feeling in her stomach. She suddenly realized how alone Claire Benson was – except for Mary of course. Mary seemed to be her only friend. And Claire was such a sweet person. Such a sweet person.

Megan looked through a bit more paperwork then decided she had done all she could at this point. Maybe she would pop into the hotel down the block for one of their famous Sunday brunches. Traffic on the street was just about nil at this time on Sunday. Unless there was a baseball or football game scheduled in the afternoon, Sundays left the downtown streets deserted. There were a few street people with nowhere to go lounging in the bus shelters or along the corners. She walked briskly down the street and entered the glass front doors to the elegant lobby of the hotel. The tall glass panels let in the sun and the tall greens almost made the area feel like a lush tropical garden. She passed the front desk and meandered on toward the courtyard restaurant in the center of the first floor. There were two layers of tables – down on the main floor by the buffet style pans of hot food and the upper balcony that circled the floor along the outside edge of the cobblestoned area. She took a seat directly below the balcony back in a corner surrounded by potted tall grasses. The waiter asked if she would like coffee with her buffet. Yes, with cream. Then Megan headed hungrily toward the line of food. There was no one in the line at the present time. In fact there were very few people seated anywhere in the area. So she could take her time without feeling a rush to decide. Taped piano music tinkled gently in the background creating a relaxed atmosphere – an oasis from the street just outside the front door.

Megan picked up a warm white plate and began to survey the selections. She glanced up toward the balcony and noticed a couple in the corner. The man had his back to her, but the woman looked familiar. She was wearing a stunning wide brimmed straw hat with cherries and white flowers along the red ribbon beneath the crown. Of course she would notice someone wearing such a hat! But the face below the hat looked familiar. Oh, yes. It was Annie St. Germaine. Her long dark hair floated over her shoulders in full puffy curls. Her white skin contrasted with her red lipstick and dark lashes. She didn't notice Megan below filling her plate with breakfast items. Annie was in deep conversation with the man across the table from her. Megan smiled remembering their meeting the previous day. Annie had indicated she was going to get married soon. The man must be her fiancé. Annie was reaching out to grasp his hand and gaze into his eyes. Ah yes, this must be the man.

Megan selected her eggs, a few slices of crisp bacon and a gooey looking caramel roll with a pat of real butter on the top. She scooped a touch of salad in the corner of her plate so she would feel justifiably healthy. Then she put a few strawberries and a chunk of pineapple on the plate as well. She could always go back for seconds. Her plate was mounding with food.

Breakfast was lovely and the coffee refilled quickly every time she set the cup down. There must be very little to do this morning with the attention she was getting from the servers. She smiled with pleasure as she anticipated going back to the dessert table for a look at the goodies. She had spotted a chocolate cake that looked tempting and the cream puffs looked light and fluffy. As she sauntered toward the table, she glanced up to where Annie St. Germaine had been sitting. She was just standing to leave and as the pair turned to the side to walk away, Megan froze. The man with Annie was Jim Peterson. And the two were indeed arm in arm as they walked toward the staircase. Megan scurried back to her table and ducked down behind the greenery as they passed. They were laughing and holding hands. And yes, Annie was wearing a sparkling ring on her finger. Megan hadn't taken the time to notice that the day before - probably because everyone who came up to the dance booth had sported a ring of some kind. After all, that was why most were at the show – they were newly engaged. Jim Peterson! Was he the one Annie St. Germaine was engaged to marry? It appeared to be so. She peered out from behind the tall fern and watched them meander toward the front door of the hotel safely out of sight.

She wouldn't let this latest development stop her from her quest for dessert. After putting a few selections on her plate she began to ponder the situation. She took a bite of the tempting chocolate cake and let it slowly melt in her mouth as she pondered the situation possibilities. Jim Peterson hadn't been present when the studio staff had found Edward's body. Nor had he been present when they were interviewed by the police about the incident. Did he even know about Edward's death? Or had he been involved in the death? Edward Garrett would certainly not take kindly to news that one of his former and potential students was now engaged to a staff member. This was strictly forbidden. But would this make a man so kind and gentle as Jim Peterson kill someone? Megan thought not. No, Jim Peterson would not be involved in Edward's death. But it made Megan think just a little harder as to who could have been involved. This was puzzling. She finished the last forkful of chocolate cake, took a final sip of coffee, and headed out to the bus stop to find a bus to take her back home. Another half hour wait would certainly be in store before the one she needed would appear – more time to think through the grueling weekend events.

IX.

Megan stood at the front door to the studio bright and early on Monday morning with key in hand as two policemen waited behind her to enter. This was expected considering the circumstances. She sighed in anticipation of the many interviews they would conduct this morning – including her own. The two men looked around the studio with an air of curiosity. They gazed at the reception desk immediately front and center as they entered. Then to the right was the small reception area with the couch and two chairs along with the coat stand. Circling behind the reception desk was the vast wooden dance floor edged along the windowed wall with glass tables and wrought iron chairs. The morning sun streamed in creating a brightness throughout the ballroom and a glistening glow to the polished floor. To the left was the door to Edward's office and then the hallway toward the restrooms and teacher offices. Megan waited as the pair looked around briefly taking in the atmosphere. The stared at the plaques and photos gracing the walls and activities board.

Carson came through the front door. Not a morning person, he had recognized the need today to get into work as early as possible. He wore his black sport jacket over pin striped dress pants and carried a coffee along with a tie. He set the coffee on the top of the reception desk and brushed back his dark hair grimly nodding to Megan. "How was your day yesterday?" he flipped through the spindle of messages from last week. She just smiled back.

"We'd like to ask you to listen to something if you could," one of the policemen interrupted and reached into his pocket pulling out a small tape recorder. You don't see many of those things anymore – not with technology the way it is today. But he had a tape recorder in his hand and motioned for them toward a table out on the floor. The four of them sat around the glass top and listened as Amanda Garrett's voice sounded.

"I met Edward when I came into the studio to learn a bit more about ballroom dancing. As a model, I attend a fair amount of social events and didn't want to look like an idiot when dancing." She laughed as she emphasized the word "idiot". "He spotted me one afternoon when I was in for my lesson. The afternoons tend to be slower, so I was probably the only student out on the floor. Of course he was drawn to me. Edward was always drawn to women who were tall and on the thin side. I guess I fit that profile." Again she laughed. "He invited me to join his morning exercise group. As a model who is trying to stay in shape, I thought this was a great opportunity. I really enjoyed the exercises and the dancing it provided. We began to see each other socially and eventually got married." There was a slight pause. Remorse? "Edward Garrett was a man of many talents. He had charisma and personality and made me laugh. He also had his faults. In fact he had lots of faults. But it is easy to overlook those sometimes. Maybe I made a mistake by ignoring some of those flaws because it caused both of us a lot of pain. I was in pain, and Edward was in pain. He recognized he had made a mistake and was trying to make amends when this tragedy happened. If Edward hadn't died, I think we may have gotten back together again." Again a pause. "Yes, I know we would have been together again." The tape ended with a loud click.

"I'd like your reaction to this statement, please." The first policeman – the one who had interviewed the group at the scene of the murder made this request. The other stood silently behind him watching for facial and body responses to the question.

Megan looked at Carson. They seemed silent for a moment taking in Amanda's remarks. Megan began first. "Yes, I would say Amanda is quite correct about her assessment of Edward and his character. She is probably also correct when she states they would have gotten back together again. I believe they would have remarried." Carson nodded his agreement as he stroked his mustache and cocked his head slightly to the side as if intently listening.

"So you are saying Amanda Garrett is accurate in her statements?" The policeman frowned as if he hadn't quite believe Amanda Garrett.

"Oh, yes. Most definitely," Carson chimed in his agreement. He pursed his lips and nodded his head vigorously.

"Edward and Amanda…why did they divorce?" He sat on the edge of his seat waiting most likely to see if the pair would come up with the same reason Amanda gave. His chin jutted forward.

"Well, I certainly wasn't personally present during their discussions or arguments as may be the case…but, I think Edward was involved with another woman – a friend of Amanda's." Megan let a grim smile cross her face.

"And that would be …?" The policeman fished.

"Ashley Dobbs." Carson interjected this answer.

"And where is Miss Dobbs at the moment?" The officer's lips pursed and he gripped his pen to take a few notes.

"We have no idea really," Megan looked to Carson who shook his head. "Edward sent her to teach for another studio owner in New Orleans. A friend of his I believe. And we heard she had a breakdown of some kind. You could contact the other studio or maybe her mother, Laura Dobbs who lives in town. I could give you her address – I don't know if I have a record of her phone number as the mother was not one of our employees." The policeman nodded his approval of this plan, and Megan went to the desk to find the number for them.

"Who else would you consider to be upset or angry with Mr. Garrett?" The second policeman swung his head toward Carson for an answer during Megan's brief absence.

"Wow," Carson pulled back at the question. "There could be lots of people – former employees, students unhappy with the studio, and personal friends. I don't know if I could give you any names of friends. He didn't confide much in me about his private life."

The first officer raised his eyebrows and breathed in a deep gulp of air. He was probably hoping for more from them.

As the rest of the staff meandered in for their work day, the officers waylaid them for individual interviews about what they knew regarding Edward's personal life. It appeared no one had much to say because the two left rather quickly although not before Megan asked if they had any information about Claire Benson. They didn't. They also slapped a card down on the top of the desk in case anyone remembered anything more to report.

"Carson," Megan waved him close to the reception desk. "Do you remember we have our Summer Festival show to do in about two and a half weeks?"

Orchestra Hall and the city's own orchestra presented a week-long festival every summer based on the Viennese Waltz. The evenings were filled with concerts featuring guest conductors and nationally known soloists. The plaza was rimmed with food vendors and booths for those meandering outside unable to get a sold out ticket inside the hall. The music was then piped outside for those wishing to sit and listen in the sometimes warm and humid Minneapolis summer weather. Each year the studio performed a Waltz for the middle week show out on the plaza. In the beginning, Edward would choreograph a new routine every year – sometimes a lofty task. But at Carson's suggestion, they began a few years back to use the same routine over again for each festival. It allowed the long term teachers to help the novice dancers learn the routine more quickly, and made Edward's life a bit easier. With two and a half weeks until the festival, they would have to begin rehearsals immediately.

"We've got just a bit of a problem," Megan continued with a grimace on her face. "With Edward gone and Claire missing, we're short people to dance." She counted down the staff members – Carson, Paddy, and Jim for the men. Megan, Sydney, Mary and KC for the women. They were missing a man to give them at least four couples. And four couples was a short number in itself.

Carson sighed. "Call a couple of our former teachers and see if they want to do the routine with us. They already know the dance. Maybe they'd enjoy doing this again as a tribute to Edward. I'll bet they haven't yet heard about his death."

Megan grinned. Great idea. She paged through her files to find a few names. Chandler Dane and Rick Krist. Those two looked like possibilities. She dialed Chandler first. He was a tall scarecrow of a man with an amazing sense of humor. Looking like a nerdy refugee from a third world country, Chandler was about six three and one hundred twenty five pounds. His short cropped hair and wire rimmed glasses provided the "nerdy" part of his look. He had remained in the training class for months bringing laughter to staff and students alike. Edward had been hesitant to make him an official "teacher" because he just didn't fit the profile Edward had in mind for his staff. Edward pictured model-like people with charming smiles and perfect bodies. Chandler Dane did not have either.

But Megan had loved Chandler and his personality as did the entire staff. She hoped he would agree to come back for the Summer Festival performance. It would be fun to see him again.

Chandler answered the phone on the second ring even though it was the middle of the day. "Hey, Chandler," Megan greeted. "Aren't you working?"

He laughed recognizing her voice. "Of course I'm working. Just not during the day! I'm doing a comedy gig at one of the clubs in town and bartending the nights I'm not making people laugh. I shouldn't say that. I'm always making people laugh." And Megan did laugh.

"You probably haven't heard yet," Megan slowed, "but Edward Garrett was murdered this weekend. At Dalton's Wedding Show."

Chandler whistled. "Wow. I'm speechless. Eddie G. dead! Murdered, you say? I'm not a suspect am I? Oh, no you wouldn't do that to me, would you? Turn me in as enemy number uno?"

Again Megan laughed. "I was just wondering if you would be interested in doing the Viennese Waltz for the Summer Festival with us. We're short a guy now that Edward's gone."

"Summer Fest? You bet! I love that routine and would like to do some dancing again. Maybe I can get some new material for my comedy routine with this one.

When are you scheduling rehearsals?" Chandler's voice was chipper and upbeat.

"For you, we'd do rehearsal during the afternoon dance sessions," Megan offered.

"That works for me! Are they still at one o'clock? You got it! I'll be there," Chandler's grin almost showed through the phone. "And Miss Meeker…I'm sorry about Mr. Garrett's death. I really am." His voice was suddenly serious and somber.

Megan Meeker sat back in her chair and smiled. It would be good to have Chandler back in the studio again even if it were only for a few weeks. Chandler had been one who was willing to do anything for a laugh. Once, Sydney had talked him into doing a 50's Swing to "Splish Splash". She was dressed like a typical teeny bopper in saddle shoes, white socks, rolled up jeans and a big sweatshirt. Chandler had been wrapped in a small towel and pink shower cap with a toilet bowl brush as his back scratcher. When he entered the dance floor for the number, the crowd went wild with laughter. Edward was furious. Once again it didn't suit his picture of a sophisticated staff to have a tall gangly man of a hundred twenty five pounds dressed in a tiny towel dancing a wild and furious swing. It had been an unforgettable experience for all who were present – and a bone of contention between Edward Garrett and Chandler Dane.

Then Megan recalled the Wizard of Oz routine he did – also with Sydney Monroe. Sydney was dressed as

Dorothy in a blue dress with a white apron, and Chandler was dressed as the scarecrow complete with raggedy clothes and straw protruding from the neck, wrist and ankles. Not that this costume was inappropriate by any means although the white face paint and red nose were quite noticeable. But that evening as Chandler was driving home – still in costume and make-up – he was pulled over for a traffic violation. The policeman found his suspect to be laughable and decided not to write a ticket. With the costume, his excuse to get home quickly seemed very plausible. Once again Chandler managed to create a few laughs.

Megan recalled last year when the studio had received a surprise call from Chandler begging them to quickly turn on an afternoon game show. The studio had a small television stored in the back teachers' office in case there was something about the studio or about ballroom dancing they wanted to show the staff and students. So they quickly pulled out the TV and flipped to the channel he requested. It was "The Love Game" and there walking up as the first contestant was Chandler Dane himself. The staff hooted as they watched the gangly man take his seat and go through a part of his comedy routine they had all heard so many times before when he was a staff member. The host began to laugh as did the date choices Chandler had to select for his dream date. The show was hilarious, and Megan smiled remembering the dismal date Chandler had chosen for his evening out. The woman was strikingly beautiful but not appreciative at all of Chandler's unique sense of humor. They had clashed immediately. When

106

their date took them to a beach setting, Chandler looked oddly out of place in his swim suit among the weight lifting crowd that normally occupied the area. Yes, it had been quite a disaster. The host of the show saw the whole event as an entertaining piece of work that brought the small studio audience to their feet with applause. They loved seeing someone else look totally foolish. Evidently that was part of the show's charm.

The staff – even the newer ones who did not personally know Chandler Dane – enjoyed the humor of the situation but also felt the heart rendering pity in chiding a person like Chandler who was a decent guy deserving a break. But Megan was sure Chandler had made the most of the situation in spite of the humiliation he suffered and probably centered his comedy routine around the incident. If he didn't, he certainly should have. It was truly a unique experience.

Megan meandered over to the costume closet in the reception area. The door to the costume closet was always closed because to open it would require too much work to get the mounds of costumes back into that closet again. As soon as Megan opened that door, the fabric began to spill out – dresses, tuxes, and an odd assortment of hats. In the beginning, a local dress designer who had never worked with dance costumes before had sewn a set of dresses commonly referred to as the "pumpkin dresses". The tops of the dresses had been way too large for most of the women on the staff and the skirts were round shaped with no flow or twirl when moving. The fabric was a heavier cotton that required the wearer to cinch in the waist to have any shape at all, and when cinched in resembled a round pumpkin. There were also the "good" pumpkin dresses and the "bad" pumpkin dresses – those added later when the staff numbers grew to a larger size and required more costumes for this performance. The "bad" dresses were even more shapeless and if possible, even more pumpkin shaped when belted. If you were assigned one of these, you were indeed at the bottom of the food chain. It was a total and complete insult! Megan herself had faced this situation several times and grimaced each time she spotted one of these wretched dresses.

When Amanda had arrived at the studio, she had put the pumpkin dresses permanently in the costume closet and had arranged for another local designer who only created dance costumes to redesign a new set of dresses for the Summer Festival performance. These new dresses were made of a heavy lycra fabric that held in any physical flaws making even the more portly dancer looking slim and trim. The scooped neckline and drop waist flattered anyone no matter what size. The skirts were three layers of a floating fabric that swirled and twirled nicely when doing Viennese Waltz turns – looking more like water lilies on a swirling current. The same fabric edged the top of the neckline so there was a softness around the breast area and a twirl along the top as well when turning. They were lovely. The soft pastel colors were elegant and flattering – yellow, pale blue, mint green, aqua, peach, pale pink, white and gold.

Megan pulled out these dresses and carefully tucked the pumpkin dresses back into the closet and quickly slammed the door closed before they could once again pop out. She hung the dresses on the hat rack and smoothed out the skirts. This fabric sprung back to shape with renewed energy and few wrinkles after a few hours. It was truly miracle fabric. The staff would have to select their dresses and practice in the gowns in order to get the lift of the skirts required during some of the patterns in the routine.

Carson came through and smiled at the dresses hanging in the reception area. "Come on and run through the routine with me a couple of times so I remember the sequence," he grabbed Megan's hand and they began to Waltz. The first few times, they had to start and stop a bit because Carson hadn't danced this routine since last summer. But Carson had a sharp mind that seemed to remember even small details about each of the dances he had ever performed. The Viennese Waltz review brought back those details. He repeated a few of the sequences alone with a bounce of his head to the beating Waltz music in the background humming along with the familiar piece of music.

Carson began to laugh when they had finally completed the routine once through perfectly. "Do you remember the year when I had to dance with Sydney, and we got stuck in the turn?"

Megan joined him in laughter. Carson and Sydney had to learn one of the routines Edward had redesigned each year, and they had only been roped into doing the routine a few brief days before the performance. Carson was sure he remembered every step even though their rehearsal time had been short. When they got out onto the plaza, following Edward himself, they got into trouble immediately. First, Edward forgot his own routine. Carson in following Edward became confused as well. Edward was doing continuous advanced left turns which were not the correct pattern at all. That was the first disaster. Then Carson had to lift Sydney, twirl her around and move from a circle formation into a straight line. Carson was not a strong lifter – in fact he was about the same height and weight as his partner. So when he lifted Sydney to turn her, it was quite a struggle in the first place. Then when the line of dancers closed and wouldn't let the pair in, Carson began to panic and twirling Sydney around and around almost dropped her right on the cobblestone plaza. He finally muscled his way into line and almost couldn't make it through the rest of the routine out of fatigue and probably a bit of fright as well. It had been at this point that Carson suggested to Edward they choreograph one routine that could be repeated year after year so such a performance as this one would never occur again. It had been a wise decision.

"I'm becoming very concerned about Claire," Carson began when Megan and he returned to sit behind the reception desk. "I think we need to really tell the police they should try to find her. It's not like her to just run off like that. Although I do admit, I know very little about her." He pondered the information he did know.

110

"Give me that card," he snatched up the business card the officer had left and dialed his number. When he was finally connected to the man, Carson voiced his concern with Claire's disappearance. Then he listened for a few moments, nodding and spouting a few "ahas".

When he got off the phone, he turned to Megan and announced, "The police are considering Claire their number one suspect in Edward's murder."

"What? That just seems so unlikely," Megan shook her head. "They must have crossed Amanda off their list after our conversation supporting her statements."

Carson nodded. "Yes, that is exactly right. Amanda is no longer on the suspect list. I wonder however, if anyone happened to mention the rest of Amanda's family. Remember how upset her father was at the wedding. He made quite a scene after he had a few drinks in him. Maybe I should have mentioned that when the officer asked about enemies."

"Besides her disappearance, what else would make the police think little Claire was capable of killing Edward and hoisting his body up with that cord?" Megan stared at Carson.

"Well, evidently they have DNA evidence that places her at the scene of the murder. The rest of us of course would have probably reason to have DNA behind that curtain, but not Claire. Not when she didn't show up

111

for the show," his manner was quiet and thoughtful. He was trying to process this information further.

X.

Rehearsals for the Summer Festival went well. Carson had paired up Jim Peterson with KC – he was experienced, and she was the novice dancer. For old time sake, he put Chandler with Sydney. The two of them had danced together so many times, it would be fun for them to reunite as partners again. He himself would dance with Mary. Again she was newer and less experienced but also they were both little people. They physically matched in height and body shape. That left Paddy to partner with Megan. Again a good match. There would be some adjustments of course. With only four couples, they would have to each take a spot – north, south, east or west in the circle and stay spaced accordingly.

The couples would line up with the women in shadow position to the man's right side. Carson and Mary would be first as the smallest couple with Mary in the tiny lavender gown. Then Paddy and Megan dressed in the yellow dress, followed by Sydney in the pink with Chandler, and then lastly Jim with KC in the mint green. The women held their skirts in their right hands prepared to wave them in and out as they cantered out to form the circle. There was a ten measure introduction to get the couples into place before beginning the actual dance routine.

Sway to the right, twirl the lady into closed dance position, and then into advanced left turns with a lady's spin in the middle. That was the beginning sequence. It was important to get the start of the routine just right because that was the first impression the audience had of the dancers. If they made a mistake in the middle, they wouldn't be quite so critical as if they flubbed the beginning. That left a lasting impression of the entire routine. So over and over they practiced the start until it became second nature.

"Let's take this out to the plaza tonight and see how the spacing works," Carson suggested after a few afternoon rehearsals. "What time does your set end tonight?" Carson looked at Chandler. "The later the better because there won't be any people hanging out down there after ten or so."

"I could get down there by 11:30," Chandler ventured as Jim groaned. 11:30? Down in the plaza on a hot muggy night? This was something he wouldn't enjoy.

"Ok. 11:30 everyone, and ladies, wear your dresses because we have the skirt work to practice as well," Carson stated with a nodded to the women.

"Ladies," Megan suggested. "Let's all just change into the dresses here and walk down to the plaza together. It's only a few blocks. Wear street shoes and carry your dance shoes. The less wear and tear on the suede bottoms the better. That cobblestone will already do a number on them as it is."

113

At 11:00 the women slipped into their pastel dance dresses and together with Paddy and Carson walked down to the plaza. Jim was going to meet them there. He had something he had to do at ten. Of course Chandler would come from the comedy club after his set.

As they walked down the street, the lights glistened in the hot, humid weather. There weren't many people still out. Most chose to be in a restaurant or pub with air conditioning. Just as they got to the block of the plaza and Orchestra Hall, Megan felt a tug on her arm. She looked around cautiously to notice the musician she and Carson had spoken to earlier about Claire's disappearance.

"Hey, lady," she sneered. "Can I talk to you for a sec." She was carrying her instrument in its case, but she still wore the peasant skirt and blouse she wore when they had spoken to her before. Her face looked tired and the sweat from the heat was beading up on her forehead and nose.

Megan left the group and huddled closer to the woman. "Remember the woman you were asking me about the other day? The one in the picture?" She looked around not wanting anyone else to hear what she was about to say.

"Yes? You remember something else?" Megan's voice began to lift in excitement.

"Yeah. I remember something else about her. She was pushing someone in a wheelchair." The woman pressed her lips together tightly.

"Are you sure about that?" Megan frowned.

"Yes. That's why I couldn't remember if she was with a man or woman because the other person was huddled in a wheel chair. They were going toward the entrance to the hall over there," she pointed with her hand not carrying the instrument case. "They was going that way."

Megan stared down her hand toward the hall entrance imagining Claire pushing a wheel chair. What did it all mean?

"Thank you. Thank you so much. I don't have any money right now," Megan showed her empty hands and dress with no pockets. "But I want to give you something. A reward of some kind. You have helped us so much. If you come down to the dance studio – the one beneath the parking ramp tomorrow in the afternoon, I'll have something to give you then. Could you do that?"

"I'm not doing this for money!" the woman stated abruptly. "I'm doing this because it's the right thing to do!"

"Oh, I know that. But certainly you could use a good meal. A nice lunch or something. It is certainly worth at least that to me," Megan was just as determined. "After all, this woman is missing. We need to find her. We think she might be hurt or lost or something."

At this, the woman pulled back with a look of anguish on her face. "Oh, my. I'll come by the dance studio, and you can take me to lunch. But I want this poor girl to be found. So I'll ask around to see if anyone else saw anything. That is terrible! Lost?" And with that, the woman turned and hurried away into the darkness. Megan had no doubt she would be at the studio tomorrow with more tidbits. She was a lost person herself who evidently didn't want anyone else to be lost either.

The whole group finally met at about 11:40. Jim was the last one to arrive. He looked tired. There were a few stragglers sitting on the benches along the plaza, but very few people walking down the street. The group lined up checking the distances they would have to move. Marking places before they rehearsed. The heat made the lycra dresses cling to the women like a second skin. Carefully, they walked around the space slowly placing the patterns in the exact spot they should be danced. After a few walks in slow motion, Carson began to count out the music at a faster pace as the four couples began to move around the cobblestone. The stone was difficult for the women with heels to dance. The thin heels caught on the ridges of stone and caused a few to stumble. "Men, catch your partners so they don't fall. This is a fast piece of music, and you need to help the women balance on this uneven surface," Carson called out into the darkness after a few frantic cries pierced the humid night air.

By the time the rehearsal was ending, the women were drenched, their dresses sticking to their sweat. The men had beads of perspiration pouring down their faces, but their casual shirts seemed to breathe better than the ball gowns. "Let's head back group," Carson finally announced to the dancers' delight. Jim raced off for his car parked along the street. Chandler waved good-by to the group as well. As the others began their trek down the street, Megan pulled Carson to the back of the pack.

"The woman we spoke to …the musician who spotted Claire on the morning of the wedding show," Megan began as Carson nodded quickly. He had seen the woman pull Megan aside.

"What did she want? Money?" he groaned assuming the worst.

"Oh, no. Not at all. She remembered that Claire was pushing a wheel chair with someone in it toward the entrance to the hall," Megan hadn't considered that someone might misinterpret the earlier meeting.

"A wheel chair? How odd." Carson was clearly stunned by this new development. What did this mean?

"She's going to stop by the studio tomorrow and let me know if anyone saw anything else," Megan continued.

"Can we trust her? She's a street person," Carson reminded.

"But she's a lost person who wants to find another lost person," Megan pronounced this with complete faith in the stranger she had spoken to earlier. Yes, she had no doubt her information was truthful.

The ladies stripped off the dresses, changed their clothes and let the wet costumes hang to dry. "Luckily these dresses wash up nicely," Megan grinned. "We may have a few more warm days and hot rehearsals, so it's good to know these are easy to care for."

Megan and Carson once again left to catch their bus home. Mary was with them at the bus stop but had to catch an earlier one as her route destination was slightly different than theirs. Megan mentioned the wheel chair while the three waited, but Mary seemed confused by this new information. No, Claire didn't know anyone in a wheel chair. Mary seemed more worried now about her friend.

The next day, Megan decided she needed to talk once again to the detective in charge of Edward's murder investigation. She pulled out his card and dialed the number.

"Yes, I've had a few thoughts about enemies Edward might have had." Megan began. "Have you interviewed Amanda's father yet? He and Edward had an argument at the wedding. I think Mr. Kihn was not very happy with his daughter's choice in a mate and would have been quite angry with Edward's affair." The officer seemed to be taking notes about this information but didn't seem impressed. Had he already spoken to Mr. Kihn and Amanda's brother and mother?

"Have you spoken to Laura Dobbs? She came in here furious with Edward when he sent her daughter to New Orleans. I'm sure Ashley's break down didn't make

118

Edward a favorite of hers either." Megan waited for a response.

After a short hesitation, the officer spoke. "Actually we interviewed Ms. Dobbs, and she has an alibi. She was down in New Orleans visiting her daughter. It seems Ashley was moved to a different facility, and the mother was helping with the move. She left for New Orleans the day before Edward was killed and didn't return until after the murder. So you see, she and Ashley are no longer suspects."

"Oh, so you had them on your list originally?" Megan pushed an eyebrow lifting in curiosity.

"We consider everyone to be suspects. But right now our chief suspect is Claire Benson who has not turned up anywhere. That is suspicious I'm sure you would agree, Miss Meeker." The officer was not unpleasant, but seemed to be a bit irritated at the turn of this conversation. It was as if Megan seemed to be questioning his judgment when she was only trying to find a lost friend and a murderer of her boss.

"By the way, do you have any idea what will happen to this studio?" Megan looked around the reception area with a new concern. Would she and the rest of the staff have their jobs?

"Well, strangely enough, Edward Garrett did not have a will. But then again, he was only in his late thirties. With his divorce, he had no immediate family. I'm no lawyer, but I think you should contact the main studio organization and see what their intentions are for the studio. It is their decision to make, I think."

Megan sighed. No one had contacted the main dance organization when Edward died. Who would have? Certainly not the police. It wasn't their job. So she reluctantly picked up the phone again and called headquarters in Washington, DC. She asked to speak with the Vice President she had met at one of the annual meetings. Occasionally Edward sent Megan as the studio representative to the national meetings. He loved to go for the social aspects of the meetings, but not for the get down business parts.

"Mr. Kensell, please," her voice sounded weak. She hadn't yet planned out what she was going to say. "Yes, this is Megan Meeker from Edward Garrett's studio in Minneapolis. We have a situation here. Mr. Garrett has been murdered." There was silence on the other end. Evidently Mr. Kensell was not the one to handle this situation. He said he would have someone call her back in just a little while. Would she remain by the phone?

Megan forgot about the street musician coming into the studio for lunch. When she showed up at the front door, she stood there transfixed staring in through the glass door not wanting or not able to enter. Megan spotted her after a few moments and called Sydney Monroe off the dance floor to the front desk. Sydney was always in early to the studio and was sitting at a glass topped table working on her programs for today's lessons.

"Listen, Sydney," Megan explained breathlessly. "I need you to sit here and work on your programs at the desk. The dance headquarters in Washington is going to call back – I just told them about Edward's death. It was a surprise to them, and they needed to discuss the situation a bit further. But I really need to take this lovely lady standing at the front door to lunch. I promised. Could you just pretend you are me and take down all the information when they call back?"

Sydney stared at the woman at the door. She recognized her as the woman who had spoken with Megan the evening before. But this whole situation was becoming a bit complicated. "Pretend I am you?" Sydney narrowed her eyes.

'I wouldn't ask if it weren't important. Really important," Megan pleaded.

Sydney agreed and piled her black hard covered programs on the side of the desk top plopping down in the swiveling desk chair behind the counter. "And I will be the best Megan Meeker that I can be," she announced with a dramatic wave of her hand and an elegant lift of her chin. "Now off to lunch with you!" She waved her hand again as if summoning a court jester or ordering a beheading.

Megan grabbed her purse – money was important - and led the musician toward an Italian bistro around the corner. The Italian restaurant called Ciscos had been in the same spot since the 1940's. The interior hadn't changed much since it first opened. It was a family owned restaurant now run by the grandson of the original owner. The floor was linoleum and the booths wooden with little carved initials along places in the wood, but the food was fabulous. In spite of the outdated décor, the portions were huge and the choices with standard Italian pastas and salads excellent.

"By the way my name is Megan," she held her hand out to her friend after they slid into a booth in the back. The musician shook the hand and replied her name was Maggie.

"Well Maggie, I'm glad you could meet me for lunch. I am trying desperately to find my friend Claire. She disappeared last Saturday, and no one has heard a word from her since. Do you have any more information? Anything at all?"

Maggie was silent as they ordered their food and beverages. Her instrument case was propped up against the seat. Then Megan decided to be more open with Maggie. She told her about the studio. How she and Claire were teachers in ballroom dancing. She told her that they were to dance for the wedding show on Saturday, and Claire hadn't shown up. She decided not to describe her about her own performance in the show's Waltz routine. After all she was not suppose to dance and had been a hasty replacement. She was also a bit embarrassed to describe the difficulties she had during the routine that careened her almost into the audience. Megan was certain Maggie hadn't seen the embarrassing clip of her on the news the other night. She would only tell the skeleton parts of the story at best.

Maggie began to relax a bit. The food arrived, and she dug in with vigor. She had ordered the spaghetti with meatballs and garlic bread. The mound of food must have agreed with her because she began to speak being especially careful not to talk until all her food was chewed and swallowed.

"I talked to a lot of people. Some of the others noticed the woman pushing the wheel chair just as I did. But the strange thing is this," and she leaned closer to Megan as if she were afraid they might be heard. "Someone else saw that wheel chair wheeled away a short time later."

Megan tilted her head to hear this new part of the story. "But the girl I saw wheeling it in... wasn't the same one who wheeled it out." Maggie chomped on a piece of meatball and reached for her cold soft drink letting the new information settle in.

"How do you know that?" Megan frowned. If Maggie wasn't the one to see the chair wheeled out, how could she be sure it was a different person?

"Because the person wheeling the chair out was old. Well, at least older. It was someone in their forties. That couldn't be our Claire," Maggie announced certainly taking a friendly view of the missing woman.

"It was a woman then?" Megan asked.

"We don't really know. The person wore a hat and clothes that could have been either a man or a woman. The person wasn't large but they weren't tiny either. So you see the problem. We don't really know," Maggie gulped a sip of drink and grabbed another piece of bread. "Could have been the person I saw earlier in the chair – I don't know. That person was also hard to decide on."

"So you say the person was about how old?" Megan returned to her age question.

"Oh, at least forty," Maggie declared with certainty.

"Could they have been older? Maybe fifty?" Megan began to probe.

"Maybe. Maybe." Maggie nodded and licked her lips for every bit of sauce.

"How old would you say Claire is?" Megan asked pondering something that flashed in her mind suddenly.

"That girl is young. Maybe eighteen, nineteen at the most."

"And me? How old would you say I am?" Megan pried hoping for a good answer.

"You? Oh, you are around thirty-five, thirty-six," Maggie smiled back with a toothy grin.

"If you must know, I'm only twenty-seven years old," Megan announced feeling a bit put off by her response.

"Well, nothing is as it seems," Maggie grinned again.

"What did you say?" Megan's voice raised a notch higher.

"I said," Maggie stated firmly, "nothing is as it seems."

"Would you be willing to check back with the witness who saw the wheel chair leave the hall and ask once more about a description and age? We could meet again tomorrow for lunch." Megan wanted more information.

"Lunch? Here?" Maggie asked eagerly with a grin. When Megan nodded, Maggie nodded her agreement. "Tomorrow?" And Maggie pointed at Megan before scurrying off with her instrument in tow. She pulled out her purse and gladly paid the bill. The information had been well worth the price of lunch.

Megan Meeker entered the studio much to Sydney's relief. In fact, she practically jumped out of her seat when she saw her pull open the front door."Thank God you are here!" Sydney was breathing heavily. "Corporate called for you and of course I pretended to be you," Sydney was rattling off the words at a quick clip. "They were sorry that Mr. Garrett was dead – murdered and all. They asked a bit about it but I told them I didn't have many details. I hope that was a good answer to give." Sydney took a deep breath and started up again. "They are looking for a person to buy the studio so we would have a new owner," Sydney began to look concerned as did Megan. Her face went into shock mode.

"A new owner? Why couldn't we just buy the studio franchise ourselves – us, all the staff?" Megan let her thoughts surface as she stroked her jaw line.

"Well, for one thing," Sydney answered back. "It takes a fifty thousand dollar investment from a potential owner to even be considered for ownership."

"Well, that kills that idea," Megan moaned. "I don't suppose you have an extra fifty grand lying around?"

Sydney just laughed at this. "Sorry to talk and run, but I have a lesson in about five minutes. Have to make that fifty thousand one buck at a time, you know."

Megan waved her off and sat down at the desk with a huff. Her fingertips rapped nervously on the wood. A new owner? A forty year old in a wheel chair? What next? But Megan began to think about what Maggie had said. "Nothing is as it seems." What exactly did that mean? Megan pulled out the employee files and paged through until she reached Claire's. She scanned the sheet again. Employees weren't required to put down their birth date anymore, but they could if they so chose, and most did because they didn't think about age as being a detriment in their hiring because of course everyone here in the studio was young. If they were older, it might be something they wouldn't want to divulge. She slid her finger down the page to birth date. So, it appeared Claire was older than Megan had first believed. Megan thought Claire must be twenty-one or twenty-two because she looked young and she spoke about just graduating from the University. But Claire Benson was in fact almost the same age as Megan. She was twenty-six. She must have started college late and not right out of high school. Hmmm. That was interesting that Maggie had thought Claire was still a teenager. Yes, she was fair haired wearing a longer style just like a high schooler would, and she was slender and tiny. That always made someone appear to be younger, she guessed.

Then just for laughs, Megan paged through the rest of the applications to see how old everyone else really was. Some of them surprised her. Carson seemed, older and he was. He was actually almost Edward's age. Mary was indeed young – twenty-one. As expected; she had just graduated from the U as well. Sydney was older than Megan. That came as a surprise. Sydney seemed so youthful. Then she flipped to Ashley Dobbs' application and gasped in shock. Ashley Dobbs, the high school student, was actually twenty years old. She was attending an alternate high school when she was hired on as a teacher. Megan practically jumped out of her seat. She looked around for Carson.

Carson was lounging in the back teachers' office. "Hey, I have to watch the desk! Come up here quickly. I have something to discuss with you." Megan made her demand sharply and quickly scurried back to the desk in case Corporate called back again. She couldn't miss another call.

"What's up?" Carson sauntered to the desk and peered over the top. Megan had pulled up a second chair squeezed behind the desk and patted the seat for him to come sit down.

He looked curious as she tried to calm herself. First she told him about headquarters trying to find a new buyer for their studio. His face fell. This was not good! A new owner? Anything could happen with that situation. They could have someone fabulous – then again, they could have a real loser who could make their lives hell. He shook his head and stroked his mustache as he did when worried.

"Let me ask you a question?" Megan let her eyes scan the ceiling. How was she going to ask this? "What do you think about Laura Dobbs?"

"What do you mean, what do I think about Laura Dobbs?" Carson was not expecting this question at all. His dark eyebrows raised suspiciously.

"Tell me what you think about her as a person? What characteristics do you associate with her?" Megan sat back in her chair and stared at Carson's puzzled face.

"Well, she seems to be a gold digger. She lives off her daughter's income as a model. Doesn't appear to have a job of her own. She would be someone who could take advantage of any situation possible to get a few extra bucks. She's one who would have pretty expensive tastes it seems. She came in here dressed in the latest fashion but doesn't work – that doesn't really make sense. I always assumed she was collecting lots of alimony from a past husband or two. That about sums it up." He looked back at her with a questioning look.

"Well, Maggie – the street musician said something interesting today. She said nothing is as it appears. So I began to think. All of your conclusions are those I would have thought about Laura Dobbs. If she was such a gold digger, why did she come in here yelling at Edward when he sent Ashley off to New Orleans when their affair was revealed? Why didn't she try to get money from him for underage sexual contact? She could have had him arrested if she was so angry or if she wanted to get a little money from this she could have filed a law suit. Or even tried to blackmail him for money not to file charges against him." Megan grinned.

"Yes, I guess that would be what I would have expected from her," Carson slowly agreed nodding his head up and down.

"Well, Laura didn't do any of this, but that's because things aren't what they seem to be. Ashley Dobbs is not a minor. She is actually twenty years old and not the little teeny bopper we expected. She was attending an alternative high school – that's why we thought she was younger. So what would you expect she was doing at twenty years old and still in high school?" Megan threw out this new question with a tilt of her head.

"She could have gone back to school because she dropped out. She could have gone back because she took time out to have a baby. She could have gone back to school because she was in drug rehab from an addiction problem...", Carson began to go down the list.

"She could have gone back because she had mental issues long before she came here to the studio...", Megan dragged out her conclusion. "She could have had a break down not because of anything that happened with Edward, but because she was a nut case already."

Carson nodded at her blunt conclusion. Yes, that would make sense. Nothing was what it seemed. Then Megan told him about her conversation with Maggie about the wheel chair and the mystery person pushing the chair. She told him the truth about Claire's age. She looks young but is actually in her mid twenties. The policeman said Laura Dobbs was in New Orleans during Edward's murder. She was down moving Ashley to a new facility. Megan suggested they do a little sleuthing on their own. She suggested they check on Ashley's condition and just where she was. Carson agreed. After all, nothing is as it seems.

The phone rang. Megan stared at it for a moment and let it ring twice before answering. It was indeed Corporate calling back. It was in fact the president himself. Megan didn't say much – just listened and then grabbed a pen to take down a few notes. "Thank you very much, and we will let you know when the funeral will be held. The body has been held for autopsy of course. In a murder case, that sometimes takes a bit longer. Thank you again.

130

Good-by." She hung up the phone and turned to Carson with a pursed sour look.

"They have a new owner for us already. That was fast! They must have had this request long before they had the news about Edward's death. His name is Barney Taft. Ever hear of him?" Her fingertips rapped again on the top of the desk.

Carson was a certified dance judge and had lots of contacts in the dance business. He frowned and shook his head. Barney Taft? No one he knew. He pulled out the national directory from the lower drawer and began to page through looking for anyone named Barney or Taft. This could take all afternoon.

No Barney Taft on the list. But Carson's curiosity got the best of him, and he looked up the name and number of Edward's dance friend in New Orleans. Then he gave him a call. After explaining who he was, he gave him the bad news about Edward Garrett's death. The friend was indeed shocked. Carson asked if the name Barney Taft was familiar – it wasn't. Then he asked about Ashley Dobbs. How is she doing? What is the name of the hospital where she is staying? He appealed to the man as a friend of Ashley's to give him further details about her breakdown. Interesting.

Now Carson had some news to share with Megan, but first another call to the hospital. Carson asked to speak with accounting and told them he was Ashley's employer in Minneapolis. He needed an address to send out personal and important financial information. That was when he discovered, Ashley Dobbs had indeed been transferred to a different facility. When he made a call to the new hospital, he was told Ashley was a new patient receiving treatment from their facility. The date given as her arrival date was the day after Edward's death. She didn't appear to show any improvement in her condition, but had only been there a short while. The supervisor was cheerful and positive wanting to give an upbeat report.

The afternoon rehearsal went well. Carson was able to take a few moments as the dancers lined up to share his new information with Megan. What did it all mean? It appeared to give no new information at all but there was something here that clearly was interesting. What was it?

"Chandler?" Carson motioned at the end of rehearsal. "Do you have time to rehearse on Saturday?"

"Hey," Chandler replied in a loud voice so the group could hear. "Why don't you all come down – oops, up – to the comedy club Saturday night after rehearsal? I'm doing my set around 10 or 10:30."

The group nodded. That would be fun. All seemed enthusiastic about the plan except for Jim who bowed out gracefully with an excuse about a family gathering.

Saturday rehearsals were fun. Easy, relaxed. No students to come in expecting a dressed up staff. No time limits on length of rehearsal. They could just dance until it was all done. Jim, of course scurried off as quickly as possible when it all ended, and Chandler headed down to the club early.

The comedy club was in the uptown area. It looked rather nondescript with no sign out front – just normal store front windows next to a small neighborhood bar. The group met first in the bar. When Megan arrived, Carson and KC were already occupying a tall round table in the back. Megan slid into a stool next to KC who was flamboyantly dressed in a billowing blouse with large navy polka dots and a tight skirt with a slit up the front. Her hair was spiky and red which looked even more so against her pale white skin and brightly rouged ruby cheeks and lips. A tall glass of ale sat in front of KC, and Carson had his glass of deep red wine. Megan looked around at the old fashioned tables and chairs spaced around the room and the bar lined with miss matched stools. Sydney waved from the front door and stopped at the bar to grab a drink before joining the group.

"So where's Paddy?" Megan asked as Sydney scooted her chair closer to the table.

Sydney shrugged. "I don't know. He's probably lifting weights like he always does Saturday evenings. Oh, and Mary called to say some relatives dropped in unexpectedly. She won't be coming." Sydney sipped her white wine and stretched back in her chair. "This is a quaint little bar, isn't it?" The patrons at the bar itself seemed to be regulars. They leaned over the edge of the wooden trimmed bar top nursing beverages not even noticing the person leaning over on either side of them. It

133

was as if they wore blinders. The bartender wiped down the counter and stacked glasses from the clean tray ignoring the droopy eyed patrons staring at the speckled countertop.

In the corners at the tables, patrons of the comedy club were having drinks before the show started. There was laughter from those tables and at least some semblance of life.

"I'm pretty excited to hear Chandler's set," Sydney was saying as Megan picked up a menu with the specials listed. "Ooh, that looks good," Sydney pointed to the back cover with a minty green ice cream drink on the cover – a sprig of mint draping across the lip of the glass.

"It does, doesn't it?" Megan decided on a hard lemonade and a basket of tortilla chips with a salsa side. The frothy mint drink just didn't seem like something this bartender was used to making – not with this crowd of patrons.

When the other tables seemed ready to move to the comedy club, the dancers got up, downed their last sips of beverage and snagged a couple of remaining chips before following the rest of the crowd. The comedy club itself was dark and actually quite small. There was a small stage in the front with a microphone stand. The tables were close together making the atmosphere quite intimate. The announcer greeted the audience and introduced the first comic. It was an older woman with gray hair pulled back into a bushy ponytail and a pair of farmer overalls. She didn't seem one bit nervous – must have done this hundreds of times. She started with a few jokes that weren't funny but ended with a few humorous lines. She thanked the audience and sauntered off as Chandler Dane took the stage.

He picked up the microphone and introduced himself, pushing his wire rims back up his nose as he spoke. He smiled in his wide grinning way and rubbed his short cut hair as if it would bring him luck. After a few feeble attempts at humor he announced, "I'm a ballroom dancer!"

The crowd looked at his tall slender frame and nerdy appearance and began to laugh. "No, really I am. I'm going to be performing at Orchestra Hall for the Summer Festival this week." The crowd burst out in laughter. "I'm dancing the Viennese Waltz. For those of you not familiar with the dance, that is Fred and Ginger meets the Keystone Cops." As he started doing a fast, stilted robotic dance, the crowd laughed even louder. "My lovely partner is right here in the audience. Stand up, stand up!" He motioned for Sydney who reluctantly stood up as the audience applause encouraged her action. Her face turned a scarlet color evident even in the darkness of the room. "Really, she is a lovely partner, but she makes me do some pretty strange things when we dance. For example, once she had me dance to a fifties rock song wearing only a bath towel wrapped around my middle." The crowd howled. "The audience was quite shocked when I first came out on the floor, but they really began to appreciate my performance when I began to scrub my back with a toilet bowl brush." At this the audience began to laugh even harder. "So my partner says to me," he began shaking his head, "is that thing clean? And I said, of course, it's been in toilet water!" The crowd clapped wildly as he waved back at them and thanked them. Sydney sat down with a thud feeling a bit embarrassed as the rest of the room began to look over their shoulders at her now that she was a part of the joke.

"He was rather funny," Megan smiled and poked Sydney who was trying to look smaller and smaller – unsuccessfully. KC was still laughing heartily and nodding her head. She hadn't been present at the studio when the actual Chandler/Sydney routine had taken place or she would have known the real performance was much funnier than the brief story just told.

When the show was over, Chandler joined the group outside the club. They all praised him for his set. He nodded a thank you and pointed to his old Buick parked along the street. "I know you all take the bus. Want a lift home?" Sydney and Megan nodded gratefully. KC said she had her own car and would drop Carson off at his house as it was on her way. Sydney and Megan piled into the car with Chandler pushing aside folders and boxes of stuff to make room to sit down on the worn cloth seats. They were all settled in when Chandler revved up the car.

"Sometimes it takes a few tries to start this baby up and running," he said in explanation. Then pulling out of the parking spot into the narrow side street, he nodded an approving smile. "There you go baby," he whispered as he glided down the street patting the car dashboard affectionately. Suddenly a figure seemed to leap out from behind a parked car. The person fell right into the side of the car plastering a dark face against the window where Megan sat. She screeched loudly as the man slid down the side of the door and onto the street next to the car. The car had been traveling at a slow speed, so Chandler put on the brakes and stopped the car leaping from the driver's side to see what had happened. Megan rolled down her window and peered out at the man lying in the street. It appeared he had come out of the corner bar before emerging from behind the parked car. His thick body was dressed in well worn clothes – heavy work pants and a long sleeved flannel shirt.

As Chandler circled the car, a group of friends or relatives of the victim emerged from the same bar and seeing their comrade in the street assumed the worst.

"Hey, what you doing?" one of them called out and began to weave toward Chandler who stopped in his tracks and stared at the crowd that was beginning to form. They began to rush at Chandler – although swaying in a drunken manner that impeded their progress. Chandler raced back around the car and leaped back into the driver's seat as the group tried to surround the car still in the middle of the street. Megan quickly rolled up her window. The crowd began to rock the car up and down chanting something that sounded more like a groan as they pounded on the windows with their fists. Chandler and Megan in the front seats huddled together toward the middle of the car seat avoiding the windows in case one of the thudding blows actually broke through the glass. A police car with siren blaring and red light flashing pulled up and pushed the crowd back to get to Chandler's window.

"What happened here, buddy?" the officer asked as Chandler stuck his head out. He explained that a man had come out of nowhere and ran into the side of his car.

The officer nodded reluctantly and asked, "You been drinking mister?"

Chandler shook his head furiously. "No, I just did a comedy set at the club over there." He pointed to the comedy club, and the officer craned his head back to look at the location of the club.

"So where is this victim?" the other officer asked as he circled the car. The crowd was pushed back onto the curb, but there was no longer a man lying in the street. Everyone in the crowd shook their heads with puzzled looks on their faces. They must have paid so much attention to Chandler and his car that they had missed the drunken man get up and stagger away. They couldn't even say what the man's real name was – only his nickname, Stinky.

At the mention of the name, the two officers began to smile. They leaned into Chandler's window and said with a grin, "We know who Stinky is, and he's probably unhurt and most likely unaware he hit a car – or was hit by a car. But if you had been drinking, we would have had to take you in. Understand? You are mighty lucky. Now drive home carefully." Then they tipped their hats to a somber and frightened Chandler Dane. A few of the crowd continued to shake their fists at the car as it drove off, and Chandler muttered, "You always get me in trouble!" Chandler pouted glancing back at a red faced Sydney. She knew he was again referring to her.

"Stinky was not my fault," Sydney piped up. "And besides, I seem to have given you lots of material for your comedy act."

As he dropped Sydney off he mumbled, "I guess this would be another piece of material I could use for my bit." His mind seemed to churn as the thought of how to turn this new episode into a comedy tale circled in his head. The edges of his lips turned up into a crooked grin.

"Yeah, you could say 'I hit a drunk the other day...'" Sydney began the monologue with a Groucho Marx tap to her imaginary cigar and a quick up and down movement to her eyebrows.

Chandler had to laugh. "Yeah, I could."

"Well, thanks for the ride and have a good evening – at least a better one than you've already had!" Sydney chuckled as she raced to her doorway. "Drive carefully!" She added as he drove off craning his neck in all directions before pulling away from the curb.

XI.

Megan met again with Maggie and tried to pump her for any more information about Claire. Age didn't seem to be something Maggie zeroed in on. After all, Maggie's own face was worn and wrinkled from a hard life on the streets, and she was the same age as Megan – well, close enough. Yet Maggie appeared to be in her forties or fifties. No, age didn't seem to be something Maggie could determine. It made Megan think more and more about what Maggie had said at the first lunch meeting – nothing is ever as it seems. Megan decided this was very true in both the case of Edward's murder and Claire's disappearance. And now they would have to contend with a Barney Taft – whoever that might be. Well, not to be concerned just yet. The staff had other things to worry about like the Summer Festival. The daily rehearsals were going along very well. They were almost to the end of the routine, and it appeared the four couples would be able to perform a nice Viennese Waltz together.

Wednesday was the night of the performance. The dresses had been freshly washed and hung in the teachers' office, the evening's late lessons had been rescheduled, and hopefully, there would be lots of studio students attending the show. They had certainly made enough announcements about the performance information. Megan was going down her list making sure every detail was in order when the front door sounded. She peered over the reception desk to see a wheel chair. Yes, a wheel chair roll into the studio. She stood mouth opened thinking immediately about Claire and the information Maggie had provided. Could this be the person Maggie and her friends had seen?

In the wheel chair was a slight dark haired man. There was no mistaking this to be a definite man. That puzzled Megan. The man had dark curly hair, a tanned Italian appearance to his chiseled face, and neatly pressed black suit. Behind him was a woman. She didn't push the chair as it was electrically powered, but she was standing alongside as if a guard of some sort. She was also slender and dark, but she wore a somber glare to her expression. Her eyes were hauntingly hollow.

Megan smiled and introduced herself. "Hello, I'm Megan Meeker, the studio manager," and she rounded the desk to extend her hand to the man.

"Hello, Megan Meeker. I am Barney Taft, the studio owner." Megan's mouth gaped open. She had forgotten all about the headquarters information on the new owner. With the Summer Festival rehearsals, she had completely put this concern out of her mind. Now here it was staring right at her.

Mr. Taft introduced the woman at his elbow as his wife, Gigi Taft. The lovely Gigi didn't seem quite so excited as she glanced around the studio with quick clips of her head. Her long dark hair was 40's style with a heavy side bang and sleek to the shoulders where it rolled under nicely. She wore a fitted navy suit with heavy shoulder pads, gold braiding and metal buttons. Her shoes were pointy toed pumps of a high gloss leather. Her well manicured hand stroked the back of the wheel chair as she looked down her Roman nose at the smiling Megan Meeker. There was no nod or handshake nor even a word muttered from the lovely Gigi.

Barney Taft breathed in deeply. "Ah, nice fresh air. So nice to have fresh air." His spindly arms gripped the arms of his chair and his legs folded together at the knees as he lifted his shoulders to inhale.

Megan nodded. "Yes," she agreed. "Fresh air is very nice." The studio was currently empty as it was early in the day, so she lifted her head to think about what to say next. Should she explain why the studio was empty? No, any studio owner would know the reason for that. Maybe tell him about the Summer Festival? Yes, that would be appropriate.

"The staff will be dancing at Orchestra Hall plaza this evening for the Summer Festival. We typically perform a Viennese Waltz each summer for the event. We'd love to have you join us – as an observer of course." She didn't know if she should add this, it seemed so obvious, but somehow she felt it was the right thing to say.

Barney nodded agreeably and said that would be very nice. Gigi was just as stoic as before. Carson and KC scurried in and stopped to stare at the couple. Megan introduced everyone as each member of the staff arrived. Barney Taft seemed to enjoy this facing his chair toward the front door waiting for each teacher to enter and meet him. His cheerful face smiled broadly with what one could only describe as pure joy.

Carson piped up, "Where are you from Mr. Taft?" He was thinking about never having found his name in the national dance directory. His curiosity was clearly peaked.

"I am from the Washington, DC area. My uncle is the president of this dance organization." Barney Taft answered clearly with a strength to his voice that didn't match his body. Both Megan and Carson nodded vigorously. The rest of the staff had no idea what he could be referring to and clearly didn't care. But Carson cared. He cared very much. As a dance judge, he had concerns for the future of this studio and his own job. He had worked very hard to get to the level and title of dance judge. Barney Taft was not going to take away all of his hard work by being a person not interested in the success of this studio and its staff. He would make sure of that. Carson stared at the man and his wife with critical eyes. Obviously, Barney was not currently a dancer. The wheel chair made this perfectly clear. But he could have been a dancer in the past – before. Barney gripped the hand of his wife as she reached down to move his chair to a different area of the room. She wanted to see something other than this waiting room filling up with gawking young teachers who were trying to grasp the meaning of this man in a wheel chair.

Gigi Taft strolled toward the ballroom. "And do you dance?" Carson was right behind her leaning in with his question when she stopped to gaze around the room.

143

"Me? Why no, I don't dance at all," Gigi simply looked around the dance floor as if a real estate broker assessing the property. "What do you do?" he continued to question.

She looked over her shoulder at him and stated quite coldly, "Why I own studios, of course." Then she swiveled her head back toward the dance floor. He didn't need to see her expression, he knew without looking she was gloating at her response.

Barney Taft smiled at Megan. "I've read all of your reports and have all your figures with me but tell me, now is this all the staff you have?"

Megan explained about Claire and how she went missing on the day of the wedding show and as it happened, Edward Garrett's murder. She glanced around at her staff and realized that yes, they were quite small now without Claire and Ashley Dobbs. There was only Megan, Carson, Paddy, Jim, Sydney, Mary and KC who wasn't yet ready to teach. It was indeed a small staff for the number of students and the volume of sales the studio generated.

"Might I suggest beginning a new training class immediately?" Barney Taft was a master of letting his new staff think something was their idea and not his edict. Carson stood back and watched in amazement at the tactful nature of this man in the chair.

"Why that would be a wonderful suggestion! Maybe we could do some advertising for prospective teachers this evening when we perform by passing out fliers to the crowd," Megan's mind was churning.

"Splendid idea!" Barney Taft nodded his approval. "And now if I am to attend your performance this evening, I need to rest." They gave him the time, directions to the plaza, and watched as the lovely Gigi Taft followed the wheel chair out the door and to the elevator.

"I think he is quite charming," chirped Megan as Carson joined her behind the desk.

Carson was not so enthusiastic about the new owners. "I think just as your Maggie said – things are not always as they seem." But there wasn't time for more discussion of the matter. Lessons were to begin, and the show was on everyone's minds. It would be a busy day. Megan did manage to squeeze in time to print up some fliers advertising a new training class for perspective teachers. She asked interested parties to call for an interview appointment. It would be interesting to see who would respond. This was a new approach never before taken to attract perspective teacher trainees.

The evening wasn't as hot and sticky as it had been all week. In fact, it was quite beautiful with a spot of breeze. The women dressed in their dance dresses paraded down the street toward the plaza. This evening there were lots of people milling around. The plaza had a number of booths lining the area with cold fruity beverages, beer, and wine along with hot dog vendors, pastry samples, decedent desserts, kabobs, and other tasty treats. There was also the constant flood of music playing. The indoor concert was piped to the outdoors for the people unable to purchase tickets to the popular event. Some people were dressed up in elegant dresses and sparkling jewels while others were simply college looking young people in frayed jeans and t-shirts. The pubs across the street were filled with people sitting outdoors watching the activities. As they walked along the street, Megan gave each teacher a handful of brochures advertising their training classes to hand to interesting people. She had cautioned them to choose wisely – no eighty year old with a walking cane or a street person carrying their life's belongings on their back. But rather look for interesting people who seemed to enjoy the music and the dancing. It wasn't hard to do. People were swaying to the music – it was hard not to.

They saw many of their own students and waved to groups of them standing with drinks and food in hand. Then after checking in with the master of ceremonies, they lined up awaiting the start of their performance. Barney Taft was wheeled to the edge of the plaza circle corded off for the dancers by his wife Gigi. She was dressed in a sleeveless sheath of gray satin with low heeled silver sandals and strings of gray, black and silver beads around her neck. Her long hair was piled elegantly on top of her head in a very Audrey Hepburn look. Barney nodded and smiled at the dancers as they stood anxiously in line waiting to float out to the center arena. Carson tried to smile back but found himself frowning as he gazed into Gigi's cold glassy eyes. She reminded him of a doll – porcelain and smooth with no inside. Hollow.

146

The music began and the four couples cantered out to their four corners to begin. They twirled in to closed position and began their advanced left turns with ladies spins around the circle, skirts clutched in the ladies' right hands giving a water lily floating on a pond effect with the pastel colored dresses. There were spins and curtsies and then into the lift – an easy lift of the lady propping herself across the man's shoulder for support while in a stag position with the legs twirling in the air. Their skirts floated out away from the body and the audience loved it clapping politely until the lowering again to the cobblestone beneath. Megan glanced out into the crowd hoping to spot Barney Taft as she circled, but seemed instead to see another familiar face. It was only for an instant. But who was it? Why did this always happen to her? As the routine ended, there were whistles from the not so distinguished college crowds in the pub area and dainty claps from the high society ladies and gentlemen in their formals and tuxes. All in all, the routine had gone very well.

Megan Meeker, used to her share of horrible mishaps in routines, released a sigh of relief. They had made it through without a dropped partner, a fall onto the pavement, nor a frantic spin trying to get into line. All had gone very well indeed. She looked around for Barney and Gigi Taft, but they seemed to have vanished. They would certainly be in the studio tomorrow for a critique.

Maggie scurried up to give Megan a quick hug. "I knew you was good, but I had no idea you was that good!"

She pronounced with added emphasis. Megan knew she meant it from the heart. "This is my friend Fred," she turned to the hunched over man who was following her. Fred as it turned out was the man who saw the wheel chair on its way out of the hall the day Edward was murdered. Fred was scruffy with graying tufts of hair on his face and an old slouched hat on his head. He grinned and nodded but didn't say much at all. He dug his hands deeper into his pants pockets.

"Fred says the person in the chair could have been young – or old. They was covered up with a bundle of clothes," Maggie spoke for Fred. Fred didn't say anything, just looked down at the ground and pouted.

"A bundle of clothes?" Megan thought that a bit odd.

"Yeah, it wasn't a blanket or anything, just a pile of clothes wrapped around them. That's why he remembered them. He thought it strange to have this huddled person in the chair all covered with clothes." Maggie nodded her head up and down. "Strange. Just plain strange."

Megan gave her a second hug, thanked Fred, and scurried along to catch up with the dance group heading back to the studio – all except Jim that is. Jim once again had to get to his car parked along the street. How he ever found a parking place along the street was a mystery in itself. There was simply no place to park anywhere on this beautiful evening. They had managed to hand out all of their fliers and hoped to get a good response. A new

148

training class would certainly be good for the studio. Everyone was booked to the limit right now and Megan had few people with any openings for new student appointments. She was going to have to start KC out on the floor soon. Tonight maybe she would mention that to her.

KC was straggling behind Carson who was rushing faster than his usual snail pace. Her hair tonight was a bright orange – vibrant. Megan saddled up to her as they got to the studio door and asked if she could have a brief word with her. KC looked a bit agitated and almost hostile at the request, but agreed to stay for a few extra moments.

They hung up the dresses in the teachers' office, and Megan sat KC down in the ballroom for a chat. "I need you to start teaching," Megan began. KC's face lit up. That wasn't what she had expected Megan to say. Megan told her she needed to start a new training class and would begin scheduling new students with KC beginning tomorrow. "I want you to look normal," Megan stopped suddenly and stared into KC's eyes. "People get a first impression by how you look and don't always give people a chance to show their personality. So you need to have normal looking hair and not green or white or orange!" Megan pointed to KC's hair. "And believe me I know about these things because I love to do some pretty wild things with my own hair, but I have learned to adjust to this business a bit. Because otherwise you will not be a success, and I want you to be successful. Understand?"

KC nodded eagerly. Obviously she was expecting a reprimand or a scolding for not handing out enough fliers or something along that line. But to finally start teaching was a dream come true. She was the only one left from her own training class – minus Claire – to get students. Tomorrow was her day. Hopefully, the routine tonight would bring new people in to the dance studio as students as well as teacher trainees. That was KC's hope. Her eyes sparkled beneath the heavy black eye liner.

The next day Megan came into the studio early. She was hoping there would be a few calls left on the recorded phone messages, and there were. There were several calls for introductory lessons and several more for the training class interviews. She stared at her daily schedule. If she could just do some interviews today and tomorrow, they could start the new training class next week. She would also have to do the initial interviews for any new students. That is unless Barney Taft or his lovely wife were trained in interviewing. She somehow doubted that.

KC walked in a few minutes later - or rather glided in. Her hair was a dark black and slicked down close to her head. No longer the heavy eye shadow or bright cheeks, she looked very normal even wearing a pair of black rimmed glasses. She had on a conservative black pencil skirt and a nice cream colored blouse with a moderately low scooped neckline. Megan had to admit she looked lovely – very normal!

"I'm starting my calls right away," Megan waved. "Hopefully we can schedule you a few lessons. You look wonderful, by the way." KC glowed with the compliment.

Carson meandered in, and then Barney Taft rolled his way through the door. His lovely wife Gigi was not with him this morning.

"The performance last night was wonderful," he gushed. "I'm sure you will receive lots of info calls from the event," he said with a glowing smile. "Wow, I just love this chair!" He twirled around maneuvering the controls at the end of the arms so the chair sped back and forth up and down the floor.

"So this isn't your chair?" Megan stood up to take a look at the wheel chair. It was new, sleek and with lots of hand controls along the padded arms.

"Oh, no. I need Gigi to push me most days with my chair at home. But this is an electric chair, and it has all the bells and whistles. We ordered it ahead of time through one of the local medical supply stores. They delivered it to the airport when we arrived."

"Hmmm. Are there many medical supply stores in this city?" Megan frowned at this new bit of information reconsidering the wheel chair facts and Claire Benson's disappearance.

"Not really. I called only a few before I found this magnificent deal," Barney again twirled in his chair with a huge smile on his face. He was a kid again playing with a new toy. Even Carson had to smile at this one. It actually looked rather fun.

"Carson, could you take Mr. Taft around the studio while I get to all my calls. We've had message upon message this morning," Megan tilted her head toward Carson who reluctantly picked up her hint and strolled toward Barney Taft with a stroke of his mustache. He was deep in thought. The studio ownership issue now weighted heavily on his mind after the festival routine was over and done with.

Megan began to make calls and scheduled four teacher interviews for this evening as well as two new student lessons with couples who had watched the show the evening before. Then she pulled out the yellow pages to check on medical supply stores. Barney was indeed right. There were only a few stores listed. What was she going to ask? She pondered her questions. Had anyone rented a wheel chair the day before Edward's death? That sounded good. She gazed at the calendar to get her dates straight before making any calls.

Barney Taft wheeled back toward the front desk. "Get your appointments booked?" he asked using the usual studio lingo. He gazed steadily over the top of the reception counter.

Megan grinned. "I've got a few teacher trainee interviews." She looked down at the schedule for the names. "A Miss Stephanie Booker, a registered nurse. Carl Young and Annalea Montgomery. I believe Miss

152

Montgomery is an avid tap dancer. Let me look up the fourth name here. A Mr. Jeffrey Cohen," she announced tapping her note pad with the eraser end of her pencil. Barney Taft smiled back. "Excellent," he pronounced with enthusiasm. She liked his encouragement. It was a refreshing change.

The calls to the medical supply stores turned up some interesting information. Three of them had rented chairs the day before Edward's death. But the names given for the rentals seemed a bit generic. John Jones. Jane Smith. Courtney Allard. The only one that seemed plausible was Courtney Allard. However, that could be a rouse. Megan would have to come up with an idea to narrow down her search.

She grabbed the phone once again. "Hey, Chandler!" she eagerly greeted the sleepy grunt on the other end. "Thanks so much for doing the routine last night. You did a wonderful job." She listened for his mumbled response. It was early in the day for him. His shy modest self was evident on the other end but only just barely. "I was wondering if you'd like to earn a little extra money?" He seemed to perk up.

XII.

The interviews went well. Stephanie Booker was a delightful woman – tall, dark haired with an infectious smile and pearly white teeth. She was a perfect Edward

153

Garrett dance prospect because of her long legs and slender build. Her hair was pulled up on top of her head, her make-up was perfect, and she wore a sophisticated business suit with gray pinstripes. Megan loved teacher interviews when the person dressed perfectly for the dance business. It was always easier to get them into the studio atmosphere. Yes, Stephanie Brooks, the registered nurse would do nicely in the dance studio.

Carl Young was an odd one. Not quite six feet tall and bone thin, he seemed charming, however. With a boyish grin on his face, his personality was pleasant enough. That is until the little glitch in his physical abilities became apparent. He explained he had some unusual disease that only allowed him to stand on his feet for four hours at a time. He lifted his pants leg and showed Megan an oozing sore that almost made her get sick. She grimaced but sat back to look at the whole picture. He was a charming man in spite of the degusting disease on his leg. He smiled and complimented and said all the right things. Yes, he would work out nicely as well. Probably. As long as he didn't wear shorts. She would have to make that stipulation clear when he started teaching. Maybe it would be wise not to share his medical history with the other staff members as well.

Annalea Montgomery was shy and young and a typical country girl. She was average height, average looks with average brown hair, and average bland clothing. She wore character shoes! Character shoes are black dance shoes with thick one and a half inch heels and mary jane straps that are totally unflattering to any woman. They make her look as if she is wearing corrective shoes for foot problems. And that is how Annalea looked – unflattering. But as Megan listened to her massive list of volunteer work and school awards, she realized Edward Garrett would find something sweet and redeeming about her. That was the way Edward was. He always found something good about each and every woman he met. So Megan took a deep breath and offered Annalea Montgomery a place in the new training class. She hoped her tap dance talents would prove worthwhile in learning this new type of dance form.

Jeffrey Cohen on the other hand was dark and handsome and extremely outgoing. He was a musician. So four good qualities. Great so far! Megan almost drooled at the prospect of a trainee like Jeffrey Cohen. He was Mr. Perfect! Unfortunately, with Mr. Cohen's band schedule, he was unavailable in the evenings. Megan had to explain that evenings were the prime time for dance lessons – for training time as well. So he would be unable to begin in the training class unless he chose the dancing over his overpowering love of music. But she never closed the door on an opportunity and told Mr. Cohen to come back if he ever left his band. They would love to have him in the studio. After all, he was probably the best candidate for a ballroom teacher in the whole bunch. Sorry to say. She shook her head but held tightly to his resume and application for her files.

Just as all her interviews for the evening ended, Megan heard a light rap on her door. Now what? Barney

Taft? No, it was Jim Peterson. Jim stuck his dark curly head in and asked if she had a moment to talk.

Jim was nervous. He was tall and fidgeting and taking in deep breaths to the point he was almost hyperventilating. "Sit down Mr. Peterson," Megan began as he took the chair in front of her desk. "Are you ill? What can I do for you?"

He looked around nervously and finally spit it out. "I'm getting married," he sat back and waited for the onslaught he obviously expected.

"I know," Megan pursed her lips and waited for the next bit of explanation. She gazed across the desk top at his puzzled expression.

"You know? What do you mean, you know?" Jim sat straight up in his chair.

"I saw you with Annie St. Germaine at the hotel brunch last week. She had a diamond on her finger and you on her arm," Megan's explanation was to the point.

Jim nodded and hesitated. "Yes, well the wedding is coming up soon, and I have decided to go back to school. Medical school." He puffed out his chest with pride. There he had said it. He had said it all. "So I have to quit. " Then as an afterthought he added, "But you're all invited to the wedding, of course. It's next weekend."

Well, that should be a nice occasion. Next weekend? Megan smiled. Jim must have kept this news to

156

himself for a good long time. She couldn't imagine Annie St. Germaine would plan a wedding so quickly. No, the two of them must have had this scheduled for quite some time. Losing another teacher? She sighed. Oh, my. What will Barney Taft say to this? Diseased Carl Young was looking better and better in spite of his oozing sores. Megan put her head down on the desk and rested her eyes after Jim left. That's how Carson Hunter found her a few moments later when he came to tell her KC's new students were ready for their review.

"So what's wrong now?" he groaned. "As if anything more could happen!"

"Well, Jim Peterson is getting married, going back to school, and quitting," Megan spit out flatly and placed her head back on the desk. "Great! Just great! By the way we're invited to the wedding, and it is this weekend."

"Ok, just do this interview with our new students, and we'll figure something out." His voice was surprisingly calming. Carson never got upset about upsetting things. He was a rock.

KC had made a great first impression on her students – a couple who had watched the routine at the plaza the evening before. They said they were excited to continue with their lessons and scheduled the next one for Friday evening. Megan complimented KC who was waiting anxiously in the reception area as the two new students left with a wave to their new teacher. KC looked extremely pleased with the development and skipped off joyfully to the teachers' office to finally claim her spot in the back room. Disgusting as it was in the teachers' office, a spot at one of the old wooden desks with all its nicks and burn marks was a treasure long awaited by each trainee. KC claimed the one next to Carson gleefully placing her first student program into one of the desk drawers and arranging a few pens in a holder on the top.

Carson sat down with Megan trying to sooth some of her earlier frustration. He pointed out they now had a new training class of three, had KC teaching and selling her first set of dance lessons, and their new owner who wasn't entirely unpleasant. The time since Barney Taft's arrival, Carson had seemed distracted and nervous about the man, but tonight he seemed very relaxed and calm. Too relaxed and too calm. What had changed?

Carson explained he had been wondering about Mr. Taft and just how much he did know about ballroom dance studios. So he had called headquarters while Megan was interviewing and asked Vice President Kensell some very direct questions. The answers he received were enough to settle his concerns. First of all, Barney was indeed the nephew of the President of this dance organization and had been around this business all of his life. Although his disease was one he had experienced since birth making dancing an impossibility, he had learned about dancing as a businessman and not as a dancer. Barney's credentials seemed to be very adequate to run a large studio such as this one. Gigi Taft was another story. The two had only recently gotten married, and Mr. Kensell knew very little about the woman. She was not a dancer, nor a lifelong member of a dance family and for that matter not even interested in this business at all as far as Mr. Kensell knew. So where did that leave them? Well, now Carson had a few more questions to ask Mr. Barney Taft the next time he saw him. Carson was satisfied with this. He had made his peace with the situation.

Megan told Carson about the conversation she had with Barney about renting the wheel chair. She not only made some calls to medical supply stores to find out if any chairs had been recently rented, but she was hiring Chandler Dane to look into this matter.

"What do you mean, 'look into this matter'?" Carson peered into Megan's face and waited patiently.

"I have asked Chandler to take photos secretly of several of our key suspects and show them to the store employees to see if anyone recognizes a face," she announced smugly.

"And just who are our suspects?" Carson was now even more curious than before.

"Amanda's parents – Mr. and Mrs. Kihn – as well as her brother. Laura Dobbs. Amanda Garrett. Although I think Amanda is a long shot. I think we should also look into the possibility of Annie St. Germaine and KC." Megan spoke fast almost rambling with her words.

"Miss St. Germaine and KC? Why do you have those two on the list?" Carson reeled back a bit. They had never even discussed the two women in connection with Edward's death.

"Well, I know Annie St. Germaine and her mother were at the wedding show. That seemed odd to me. And Edward would not have looked favorably on Jim and Annie's wedding. After all, she was a student and potential money source for the studio. To Edward the money was just about everything. Then of course, KC was the only staff member from the studio – except of course, Claire Benson – not to be at the show. She is just simply a suspect because of availability. Nothing more." Megan's explanations were clear and concise. "I should also add Claire to that list, but we don't really have a very good photo to use for identification. All I have is that one old photo I carry around with me. I guess that will have to do."

Chandler had called Megan back at home the next day. He asked her to give him a few days. He was getting some candid shots of the people on Megan's list but needed time to visit all of the employees at the medical supply shops as they had several part time people working some pretty strange shifts. He wanted to make sure to get to all possibilities. Megan said she understood.

This was the weekend to kick back and enjoy some relaxation and a wedding, of course as she quickly mentally recalled. Monday they would start the new training class. The calls from the plaza show had continued to come in, so there were lots of new student appointments scheduled. KC seemed very pleased with her new busy schedule. Edward's funeral would be on Tuesday morning. Barney

Taft had announced he would be staying for the funeral, but would travel back to Washington on Wednesday. He wanted to have dinner with Megan and Carson to discuss arrangements before he left. Yes, it would be very busy. In addition to all of the studio activity, Chandler would hopefully come in with a report about the wheel chair. Oh, my. Megan took a deep breath and let her eyelids slowly close as she pondered her upcoming schedule.

Determined to hole up in her tiny apartment and get some much needed rest, Megan managed that part on Friday evening after the studio closed. She made a delicious meal of beef stroganoff for her dinner adding a glass of red wine and her favorite TV show taped from the middle of the week. It would be a delightful evening of doing nothing. Megan chuckled with excitement. She settled back for a relaxing evening.

Carson on the other hand, was enjoying another evening with his housemates plus a jubilant KC. After her first lesson taught, Carson had prudently invited KC to the weekend dinner. She was now considered a true staff member.

The group sat around the massive wooden table and shared in a meal of potato soup, fresh dill bread with whipped butter, garden greens with a raspberry dressing and hand churned ice cream. Everyone had taken a turn in making this dessert treat from a genuine crank bucket wrapped in chunks of ice and salt. The wine and beer flowed freely as the friends shared stories about a brutal workweek. This time KC could share her own experiences.

161

It felt good to feel part of the group. She had doffed her business attire and was once again spiking her hair and wearing a loose peasant dress that circled her ankles and thick wedged sandals. Her arm was clanking loudly with dangling bracelets of all colors. It was the perfect ending to a long but satisfying week for KC.

Carson was sharing his impression of Barney Taft with the group who found this quite fascinating – a dance owner in a wheel chair. One of his housemates, a doctor frowned at the animated yet detailed description of the cheerful man in the wheel chair.

"Can you describe his physical condition again?" He leaned in trying to glean a few more facts.

Both KC and Carson tried to present a joint picture of Barney's frail condition. At the end, the doctor proclaimed, "That sounds like a degenerative condition that most people of his age do not live to see. Curious. He really should not be living if he is as old as you say he is." The statement made Carson ponder Barney Taft with new concerns. What would his motivation be for buying a studio if he was in such a delicate physical state? Certainly not to present to his cold and decidedly uninterested wife, Gigi! Carson decided to ask him point blank about his health and his intentions for the future of the studio. After all, this was his career he was playing with – and the career of several other people as well.

Saturday came bright and beautiful with Megan feeling refreshed and renewed by her luxurious night at home – alone. Only a few of the staff attended Jim and Annie's wedding. It was too sudden for most to change plans. But Megan and Sydney decided to go to the event together. It was a woman thing – see the dresses, the cake, and who from the social elite of Minneapolis would attend, etc. Megan wore a simple beige dress which was most unusual for her – she loved the bright colors and flamboyant styles. But she had been just too tired that week to spend time searching through her closet for the perfect wedding attire. She simply picked the first thing she saw. And it was beige. Sydney wore a soft navy patterned dress she frequently wore for studio dance routines. It had a lovely flow to the skirt and looked like a dance dress. She clipped up one side of her hair for a more dramatic effect. Not that anyone would notice either of them. Not with all of the social elite invited to the elegant event. Not with all the magnificent dresses and baubles worn by the rest of the attendees.

Jim and apparently Annie St. Germaine as well were both very involved in the church. The ceremony was in a large and ornate church packed with people – most who seemed very familiar with this particular church. Everyone seemed to know everyone else. Before the bride and groom's families took their places in the front of the sanctuary, the attendees chatted amongst themselves as the organ music droned in the background. Women wore wide brimmed hats and light pastel and flowered dresses – perfect for a summer afternoon wedding. The men were dressed up as well in light colored suits and crisp dress shirts. There were no "college-type" friends in attendance. Everyone was spotlessly elegant.

Annie's mother and siblings walked up to the front of the sanctuary attended by an usher in a light gray tuxedo. Annie's mother was dressed in a lacy pale blue suit with a small blue netted hat on top of her dark hair. Megan recognized her from the wedding show, and noticed the striking resemblance between mother and daughter. Annie's sister and brother were in their early twenties and stylishly dressed as if attending the Kentucky Derby – matching pastel suit and dress in a pale blue shade as well. Their perfect posture looked regal and poised as they took their seats nodding to guests along the way.

Jim Peterson's parents were escorted up the aisle by another usher in gray. Megan couldn't remember if Jim had any brothers or sisters, but none sat with the parents. Both parents were tall and slender – almost angular. His mother had slight streaks of gray running through her auburn hair and his father had a cool dark gray full head of wavy hair. Megan couldn't help but think Jim would someday look just like his father. His mother was dressed in a soft green suit and his father wore a tuxedo that matched the gray of the ushers. Their faces shown with delight as their son moved stealthily into place at the front of the church alongside a twin – no, his younger brother possibly? Jim stood straight and tall waiting...waiting. His smile plastered broadly across his face. The front of the church was decorated with several very large bouquets of splayed flowers in pastel pinks, lavenders, and yellows. Everything was of course perfect.

As the traditional wedding processional began to play, Megan's mind immediately went back to Edward and Amanda's wedding. So different. Edward had given the atmosphere a sharp tenseness with his tardy and insensitive manner toward the whole event – when Megan knew it had truly been a very important moment for Edward. Jim on the other hand gave the afternoon a calm and reflective mood. His face lit with delight and joy.

The string of bride's maids began to slowly meander down the aisle – each wore matching dresses in different pastel colors. The first was yellow, the second lavender and the third pink just like the bouquets of flowers in the front. These dresses were the typical brides' maid dresses – something no one would dare wear after the wedding. They had a soft color but that shiny stiff fabric that stood out away from the body was cinched in at the waist with a matching cummerbund in a wide gathered fabric trimmed with tiny white flowers. The scooped necklines were conservative with each bridesmaid wearing a tiny gold cross on a delicate chain - probably a gift from the bride. No, Megan couldn't conceive of wearing these dresses anywhere after this day ended.

Finally, Annie St. Germaine was escorted down the aisle by her handsome father. It was plain to see Annie was indeed her father's daughter. He beamed as he guided the tall and striking bride in her traditional white gown of lace over satin and streaming veil down the plush carpeted aisle.

The guests stood and "oohed" and "aahed" as she smiled at both guests and blushing groom from beneath long dark fluttering lashes barely visible through the filmy veil. She had an air of innocence and yet the look of a very sophisticated and successful business person. Her father skillfully presented his daughter to her soon-to-be husband with great fluidity and graciousness. He took a deep breath and slid in next to his wife taking her hand gently as they glanced at each other with complete satisfaction. Jim Peterson was clearly someone they approved of for their daughter.

The ceremony was lovely – traditional and yet simple. The organ played "wedding" music and a soloist with a lovely high soprano voice sang hymns. The families and the guests were gushing with good wishes after the ceremony was over as they proceeded through the receiving line and prepared for the jaunt to the reception. Annie and Jim both seemed pleased that Megan and Sydney had chosen to attend the wedding.

"I know this was very last minute...", Jim apologized as he extended his hand for congratulations. "Please come to the reception. We'd love to see you." His smile was very genuine. Annie nodded her agreement.

After discussing the situation, Megan and Sydney decided they should take advantage of the free food. Yes, they could manage a little time this afternoon to eat and mingle. After all, it would be good publicity for the studio. They could pass out cards, and it would be a business sort of event. That was their excuse to – well – eat gooey and sugary cake! Everything could be adequately justified.

They arrived at the large reception hall at a local country club. Evidently, Annie St. Germaine came from a very affluent family who were almost the founding fathers of the club. They were greeted with great honor and respect by the club's staff. Yes, there was a large portrait of Mr. St. Germaine among the gallery of executives along one of the hallway walls. The place was magnificently decorated with all of the same pastel colors used at the church – flower arrangements on each of the small tables neatly covered with crisp white table clothes, pastel napkins and dinnerware. The long front table was scalloped with leis of pastel flowers softly outlining the table itself. There was of course the long table for gifts which was already stacked with packages in glittering paper and creative bows. A young girl was scurrying back and forth arranging the packages and creating spaces for new additions.

Ah - the cake table. The cake was outstanding – layers of pastel frosting – one layer yellow, another pink, and a third lavender with a top tier in white with a traditional bride and groom figure on top. It was circled with real flowers in the same color scheme. There was a small band playing in the corner of the room. The combo was dressed in white dinner jackets and each looked to be at least eighty years old. But they played with gusto all of the big band sounds made famous by Benny Goodman and crooner Frank Sinatra. The guests were already tapping their toes to the beat.

After a typical wedding dinner of chicken and rice pilaf, the couple was toasted with glasses of sparkling water – both Annie and Jim were non-drinkers. They cut the cake and waited for the evening's dance to begin. Jim must have been working very hard to teach Annie a few dance moves because the couple danced the first dance to a Waltz and looked elegant indeed. Jim smiled proudly as the guests complimented them on their talent and soon the dance floor was filling with prospective students. It was getting late for Megan after a long week, and she looked past the possibility of snagging a few new clients and begged Sydney to leave early.

"You look tired," Sydney commented and nodding, stood to leave the festivities. They both managed to slip out without much comment from anyone in the crowd. After all, no one other than the bride and groom really knew who they were. They were strangers in a sea of friends. It had been a long day. It had been a long week.

Monday came too soon for Megan. She sat wearily on the bus waiting to arrive downtown. Then she lumbered slowly toward the studio – still locked. She was the first to arrive. She scanned the schedule briefly and picked up her to-do list from the place she had clipped it last Friday.

First, Megan checked the arrangements in regards to Edward's funeral – a small private affair just for Amanda and the rest of the studio staff for Tuesday. It would be in a funeral home near the studio.

Second, she went through the training class arrangements that would begin that evening at six sharp. The three of them - Stephanie, Carl, and Annalea – would need constant supervision. Megan would teach the first hour indoctrinating the group to the studio itself and what to expect. Then Carson, KC and Sydney would share an hour each of teaching dance patterns. That would work out nicely.

Stephanie Booker was the first one to arrive. Prompt. Megan liked that in a teacher. Paddy O'Brien was waiting for his next student and took one look at the lovely Stephanie and fell in love immediately. Megan could tell just from the glazed over look in his eyes. Oh, no. Not another love match. She had had it up to here with love matches in this studio. Megan decided then and there to sit down with Paddy that evening for a little chat about rules and regulations and all that other good stuff. Barney Taft rolled in as well. Megan was surprised he hadn't appeared earlier in the day, but he seemed chipper and excited to meet the new training class. He announced he would accompany Miss Meeker for the first hour of instruction with the class.

The trio was a bit surprised when a smiling man in a wheel chair rolled up to join their class huddled in the back of the ballroom around one of the small round tables. Stephanie, the nurse looked curiously at his body position and tried not to react to his delicate condition. Carl and Annalea just looked perplexed.

"Hello, I'm the owner of his studio, Barney Taft. You may call me Mr. Taft. At this studio we are always professional and address each other as well as our students by their last names. That way our students recognize the respect we have for them and for each other. It is easy in the dance business to have people try to get close to us personally. So we make sure right from the start to remain professional at all times. Understood?" The three nodded and introduced themselves one at a time to Mr. Taft. He chatted with each one asking about their reasons for applying to the studio and what they hoped to receive not only career wise but personally from the dance business.

Megan Meeker sat with the group but took in all that Mr. Taft said to the trainees. He didn't say too much, but what he did say was extremely important and he was a very good listener. He made a friend of each and every one of them, including Megan Meeker.

"I have a condition that makes me physically weak. My mind is sharp, but my body is not. I have been fortunate. I come from a family with lots of dancers – very wealthy dancers, I might add. That money has allowed me all the best in care and treatments for my condition. But I am dying. I will tell you right up front, I don't have much longer to live. I know that, and now you know that. But I want you to be the best teachers, the best dancers, and the best staff this studio has ever had. Because when I am gone, my wife will own this studio. She is not a dancer.

170

Nor does she know anything about this dance business. But together, you and the rest of this very capable staff will be able to run a successful studio. I know you will be the back bone of this organization. So learn as much as you can as quickly as you can, because in a very short time, you will be needed. Miss Meeker here will need you all to be the best you can be." And with that said, Barney Taft rolled his wheel chair away and out the door back to his temporary hotel room and some much needed rest.

Megan hesitated as she watched him leave. They all watched him leave. There was a moment of silence then she turned back to the group and began the training session she had originally planned. Interesting. She had indeed learned a great deal about the mysterious Barney Taft and the future of this studio.

Jim Peterson prudently called in sick for the evening. Megan expected he had planned this for quite some time as his schedule for the week was sparsely filled, and any appointments he did have could easily be taught by any of the other teachers on the staff. Nice forethought on his part, she decided. Maybe she should have been more diligent last week when he announced his wedding but things had just moved too quickly and the thought never crossed her mind to ask about his schedule after the wedding.

XIII.

It was Tuesday. The funeral was simple. Amanda Garrett and her family were present seated in the front row of chairs. The rest of the studio staff was seated behind them. Barney and Gigi Taft were along the side so the wheel chair had a nice open spot to view the casket. Not that Barney or Gigi have ever met Edward Garrett before, but there was a nice photo blown up next to the coffin showing the smiling man in better days. They gazed on the image and nodded with a somber look of pity in their eyes. No one else attended the service. It was short and sweet with a few positive comments made about Edward and his dream for his dance studio. Yes, he definitely was a talented man. The funeral director had a nice array of cookies and brownies along with coffee in the reception room after the service was finished. No one wanted to mill around very much, but everyone politely nodded a hello to each other and sampled the sweet treats. Then it was all over.

Amanda's father had looked angry throughout the service. He pouted even when his wife poked him in the rims reminding him to be pleasant. He didn't appear at all to be a pleasant sort of person. Obviously a man of great wealth, he dressed in an expensive suit because it was socially expected. But his heart and spirit were definitely defiant and irritated. The son was aloof but not hostile by any means slouching with his hands stuffed in his suit coat pockets as he surveyed the sparse offerings on the cookie tray. He followed behind the rest of the family as both the mother and father supported the visibly upset Amanda. They would be good parents, but not good in-laws. Clearly their heart was only there for their daughter and not for the man who was brutally murdered.

Barney Taft pulled Megan to the side and asked if there was a corner where they could chat for a few moments. Scanning the area she motioned toward an alcove just outside the reception room. They were alone, and it was very quiet in the hallway. The window in the alcove was curtained with sheer panels letting in the sunlight and there was a small love seat of Victorian design in the corner beside a large potted plant making the space quite cozy and secluded. Megan sat in the love seat, and Barney rolled his wheel chair parking directly across from her.

"I will be leaving soon. I need to get back home to visit my doctors. This trip has really taken away my strength much more so than I expected." He smiled but his eyes looked tired. "I don't expect I will live much longer. The doctors have not been hopeful. I've had to live with that possibility for quite some time now, but it is evident even to me they are correct in their diagnosis. Gigi will inherit the studio. Our marriage is a marriage of convenience. She cares for me in exchange for my money and my inheritance after I am gone. But I'm sure you suspected that all along. She is a woman of great needs – financially that is. But she is not a person of warmth. And she does only what she has to for the money in the end. I don't know if she is even interested in this studio at all. I

173

bought it for her – an investment in her future. I had hoped this trip would spark her enthusiasm for the dance business, but she seems to be very disinterested. The trip has been an inconvenience for her, and she is quite ready to leave." At this point he laughed but there was sorrow in his face as well. "After all, I grew up in a family that loved dancing. She did not, I am afraid. She does not share my interest in the business. From the time I entered the studio, I knew you and your staff were people who loved the art of dance. You cared for this studio even after your boss and mentor died. You continued with what you love to do, and it shows. This studio will be very successful, indeed. I have made a difficult decision. I will try to persuade Gigi to make arrangements to sell you the studio. I know it is a stretch to think you have the money to buy it outright – not yourselves at least. But I am going to meet for dinner this evening with Mr. Kihn. I know he is a very wealthy man. Maybe he would be interested in loaning you the money as an investment. I can see that his daughter is a person who still enjoys the studio and the people in it. I may be able to persuade him to make a deal that would satisfy all parties involved – Gigi, Mr. Kihn, Amanda Garrett, and you. Would that be of interest to you?" His eyebrows raised waiting expectantly.

When his speech was complete, Megan sat breathlessly thinking about all he had said. There was a lot to think about. Yes, she did want to own the studio and no, she did not have the money to do so. Would he be able to make an arrangement that would be fruitful for her? Would Carson want to partner with her on this investment? She smiled back at Barney Taft and nodded. She had to trust he would make a favorable deal. Placing her hand on his, she said softly, "I trust you to work on my behalf just as I trust you will do so for your companion Gigi. Yes, make an arrangement for me that will keep the studio with us – the ones who love to dance and love to share that with others." She stopped speaking and gazed into his soft warm eyes. His curly hair haloed his face. She knew he understood. She didn't need to say anything more.

The staff walked back to the studio in silence. The new trainees had not been with the group. They didn't know Edward Garrett, nor did they even connect the announcement about his death on the news and in the media with the studio. Megan wanted to tell Carson about her conversation with Barney Taft, but before she could, Chandler Dane sauntered into the studio and peered over the reception desk with a grin. He looked first to his right and then to his left before placing a manila envelope in front of Megan. He loved the drama of the situation. He tilted his head and raised an eyebrow – just one. So detective-like!

Everyone was on the dance floor starting lessons or out for lunch. The brownies at the funeral were just not that satisfying for most of the dancers. Megan's own stomach growled uncomfortably with groaning rumbles. She stared down at the packet and slowly opened the clasp. Several smooth glossy photos slid out. She placed the photos in a line across the desk. Amanda Garrett was glowing with her model smile and pearly white teeth. It had been a photo taken by her own booking agency. Chandler had asked for one when he stopped in inquiring about her availability for a shoot. Megan imagined Chandler loved the acting required for that visit.

Then there was Mrs. Kihn. She was on her way out the front door and looked harried. Tiny and well dressed, Mrs. Kihn had a pinched look on her face with her lips pursed tightly together and her eyebrows in a furrowed frown. Her dark hair in the sprayed helmet style from the wedding and funeral was now straying away from her face in unkempt ringlets.

Then there was Mr. Kihn standing outside his office speaking with a partner. He looked deep in thought yet casual and relaxed with his hands slipped easily into his pants pockets. The brother/son was sitting in a café with friends. His head was back in a half laugh. He had a smoothly shaved face with just a touch of a light mustache starting to form on his upper lip.

Then there was Laura Dobbs. She had been opening her door and was peering outside. Her eyes seemed to dart from side to side even in a still photo. Chandler must have done the old ring the bell and run trick on her.

KC was dressed as she had been the evening before – professionally. It didn't really look like the real KC at all, but you could tell who it was if you had a good imagination. Her tailored suit fit snuggly on her round body.

Annie St. Germaine was sitting at a restaurant with Jim Peterson. They were gazing into each other's eyes romantically. Ah, young love. Yes, she was wearing a wide brimmed hat with sprinkles of spring flowers tucked into the sienna colored band. She had a well manicured hand gesturing with her sparkling diamond flashing with a glint in the beams of sunlight. She was a picture of socialite perfection.

"My, my Chandler. You certainly did a great job getting these photos. Now, what did you find out about them? Did anyone at the medical supply store recognize any of these?" Megan fingered a few for another glance.

"As a matter of fact, someone did recognize one of these lovely candidates!" He grinned, but it wasn't with humor. It was with a distasteful stare. "Well, almost." He added. "They said it might be the person who rented a wheelchair." His finger ran over all the photos one at a time taunting Megan's anticipation and then suddenly stopped on one of them. "This one," he said picking up a glossy print of Laura Dobbs. "Someone said this woman looks like the person who rented a wheel chair on the day before Edward's death and had them pick it up at the airport the day he actually died."

"How can that be? Laura Dobbs was in New Orleans when Edward was killed." Megan stuttered. "The police already checked out her alibi. They told me. There must be some mistake."

"Well, I'm going to take a few days off and go on vacation," Chandler announced with a great deal of enthusiasm.

"I know you've worked hard to get me this information and all, but why would you decide you deserved a vacation right now?" Megan said with a twinkle in her eye. Chandler's voice was teasing her.

"Because New Orleans sounds good right about now, wouldn't you agree?" Chandler tapped his fingers on the top of the reception desk.

Megan laughed but then looked at him somberly. "Chandler, you don't have the money to go to New Orleans. A comedian doesn't make much money. I am going to see if the studio would pay your way and your expenses," she pondered how she could arrange this.

"Just how are you going to do that?" He leaned on the top of the desk.

She picked up the phone and dialed a number. "Amanda? This is Megan. I know this has been a hard day for you, but I have a question for you. We have some information that might solve Edward's murder. But we need a little money to finance a trip for one of our staff to confirm that information. Would you be willing to help finance this?" Megan waited with baited breath for the reply. "Yes? Thank you." She turned to Chandler. "You have your plane ticket and hotel covered. Will that work?" Chandler grinned back and nodded.

"I'll call you when I get there." And he was out the door with a wave of his hand. What would he find in New Orleans? Megan felt her heart beating loudly. She had hope.

It was only a matter of moments before the bell on the door rang again, and Barney Taft was wheeled in by a glamorous Gigi with Mr. Kihn trailing behind sporting his usual menacing expression. A smiling Barney greeted Megan and asked if she had some time to meet with the three of them privately. Gigi stood erect gripping the handles of the wheelchair. For a tiny woman she had a brittle sharpness to her attitude. Her bright red heels were tall and spiked – the pointed tips barely covered by the well creased straight legged pants she wore in a deep gray with light gray pin stripes. The pants were simple and smooth accentuating her tiny hips. She wore a short cropped jacket in a deep gray with puffed padded shoulders over a soft red blouse with a neat but full bow at the neck. It was almost overpowering all of the puff and fabric for a woman so slender and delicate boned. Her dark hair was twisted on top of her head and her make-up displayed bright red lips, flushed cheeks and long black lashes. She had an ageless appearance. Megan always guessed she was youthful – maybe in her twenties – but as she stared at her smooth face, she realized she might have that appearance because of cosmetic surgery. Expensive cosmetic surgery. Her face was simply too tight and stretched to be natural.

Megan found a staff member to cover the front desk and led the trio towards Edward's office. They each chose

179

one of the comfortable chairs and Barney rolled his own chair to the edge of the large cherry desk. Mr. Kihn immediately looked around the office – probably trying to spot a photo of his daughter or possibly the woman who broke up that marriage. There was a small picture of Edward and Amanda on one corner of the desk top and his eyes stopped to assess the pose. Then he took his seat and crossed his legs arrogantly. Megan longed to stand – to hover over the rest of them but settled into a chair in the front of the desk while Gigi stubbornly chose the seat of honor behind the desk. She seemed to drown in the large overstuffed desk chair Edward had always occupied but her expression was one of powerful control.

Barney began by nodding at Mr. Kihn and smiling broadly. "We have discussed the situation in regards to this studio at great lengths and have finally come to an agreement." Pausing, he twisted his head and as much of his body as he could toward the lovely Gigi. "My dear wife is not interested in owning and running this dance studio." His statement was cheerless and blunt, his head shaking slightly from side to side. At this Gigi frowned but smugly crossed her arms over her chest as if she were put on display by his words. And she was. Both Megan and Mr. Kihn quickly turned their attentions toward her.

Barney Taft continued. "Mr. Kihn, always a man looking for a good investment, has agreed to buy the studio – no, excuse me – finance the sale of the studio to the staff. By the 'staff' I mean those who are interested in taking advantage of this business deal. I'm sure not everyone would be willing to invest in this studio. But there are some who would like this proposal, I'm sure." At this Barney turned his attentions to Megan. "Of course there would be a monthly pay back schedule we will arrange from the profits, but the maintenance of the business would be the responsibility of those interested in this proposition."

Megan cleared her throat and asked hoarsely if she could invite some of the other staff people into the meeting for the details and both Barney and Mr. Kihn agreed. Mr. Kihn grunted and folded his arms with a reluctant glare. Sydney Monroe, Carson Hunter, Paddy O'Brien, KC, and Mary joined the group to hear the proposition. The training class was of course not in yet and would not be part of the studio staff just yet. Jim was not in today after calling in sick again. Mr. Kihn grumpily pulled out a piece of paper with his numbers scribbled in neat rows. He presented the amount he was willing to finance and how much he would require each month to make the purchase.

Gigi sat smiling at the dollar figure she would be receiving from this sale and sat up in her chair flicking her crossed foot up and down. Finally, Barney asked for a raise of hands from those who were interested in buying the studio. Megan shot up a hand as did Carson. With Carson's hand up, KC lifted hers slowly as well. Then Sydney raised hers. Paddy and Mary shook their heads. They didn't want to feel tied down by the financial burden of ownership. They were both young and although enjoyed their jobs had thoughts about changes in the future. A ten year commitment seemed to be too much to consider right now. Barney nodded. He knew there would be a few who wouldn't have an interest. It was no surprise. Paddy and Mary left the room as the others crowded around the desk to negotiate and understand all the numbers. Mr. Kihn explained each entry carefully so there would be no margin for error or misunderstanding. Megan's heart beat wildly as she looked at the figures and tried to calculate in her head the profits verses payments. Was this do-able?

When Gigi Taft rolled Barney out the door an hour later, her red heels clicked loudly on the cement outside the door, and she was smiling broadly at the large check stuffed in her purse. Megan and Carson would not see the couple again. In fact the news of Barney Taft's death two weeks later sat heavily on the two of them. They had both appreciated the man in the chair after this brief but important visit. Although they had known his death was eminent, the news affected them deeply. He had truly been an inspiration.

XIV.

"Somehow, I don't quite feel like a studio owner yet," Carson admitted as Megan, Sydney and KC sat around a table in the pub right across from Orchestra Hall. It seemed a fitting location. They had decided to toast their new business and discuss some of the arrangements. Megan would continue to manage the studio, but they would need to have weekly or bi-weekly meetings of the board – the four of them to make decisions. Not that they were interested in changing everything. They were still associated with a national organization that dictated much of what they did but there were some things they could make decisions about such as prices and groups and schedules – staff policies. KC hadn't been around as long as the others, so some of the day to day running of the studio was still foreign to her. She made a choice to stay silent when it came to things she didn't yet understand. She wanted to take her time learning some of the ins and outs of this business. Trust these partners to know what should happen and what shouldn't.

Mr. Kihn had proved to be a shrewd businessman. This made Megan a bit suspicious of him and his intentions. In fact, it made her rethink her suspicions of him in regard to Edward's death. Could he have done such a thing? Absolutely. After today, she was even more convinced of his disregard for integrity and honesty in his life. The four of them would have to keep a sharp eye on the man. Even with four against one, she had the feeling they were indeed outnumbered. She wondered how Amanda Garrett had grown up with the man. Amanda's mother must truly be a saint. There are some people after all, who seem to have a nasty side that is in no way hidden away. Mr. Kihn was one of those people. Megan had grown to dislike him all the more after the hour she spent with him today. His snide remarks and fierce nature were quite evident all through the negotiations. He made her feel uneducated and stupid not just about finances but about the entire dance industry – one she had been a part of for many years. It was an irritating and gut retching moment when she realized how miserable he could possibly make this whole process.

After a few toasts and a plate of greasy French fries shared by the four, they all hopped on their separate buses and went home. It had been a long day. As Megan unlocked her front door, she thought about Chandler. She wondered if he had gotten to New Orleans and when she would hear from him again.

The next day in the studio proved to be interesting. It was their first day as new studio owners. Megan settled into the chair at the reception desk and watched as Paddy O'Brien escorted the lovely new trainee Stephanie Booker through the front door. Evidently they had gone dancing last night – together. Paddy had indeed taken an interest in the new teaching prospect and was now moving in to stake his claim. Stephanie was pulling her dark hair into a secured tail on the side of her head. It draped like a drippy faucet over her right ear. She had smooth skin with a bit of sunglow and a few freckles on her cheeks and neckline. Her deep purple sweater was scooped in front over a long black pencil skirt. The thin bones of her clavicle protruded just above her sweater neckline giving her a gaunt appearance. She didn't yet own a pair of dance shoes, but wore black high heels that every businesswoman in the downtown area wore to work. They certainly didn't look comfortable with the height of the pointy heels, and the narrow toes would have squashed Megan's feet into a painfully uncomfortable position, but they were made to be worn all day by the business executive woman trying to look her best from morning to night. So they must not be too bad. Stephanie's smile was like a grinning cat, and she was now smiling at Paddy. Paddy was tall and slender with jet black hair. His flat, round face always looked sunny and smiling. Like a cartoon sun. The slant of his eyes reflected his Asian heritage. That was the reason his name – Paddy O'Brien – always took his new students by surprise. They expected someone with red hair, a ruddy complexion and a rotund body in a green kilt.

He carefully escorted Stephanie toward one of the glass topped tables in the ballroom and raced to put on a piece of music. Then he motioned for her to join him on the dance floor for a sultry Rumba. He explained every detail of their movement as if she were a student – his voice booming across the deserted wooden floor. Megan always hated sitting at the reception desk during one of Paddy's lessons because she could hear clearly every word he said. His voice was like a sonic boom. She actually found herself covering her ears with the palms of her hands. It had become an instinct now.

Paddy's high Cuban heeled dance shoes clipped crisply across the floor as he danced with Stephanie. They were almost the same height with Stephanie in her heels, and she looked long, lean and a slightly bit hunched in an effort to appear shorter than her slender partner. But she was beaming with the attention. For a new dancer, she followed Paddy's lead very well. He was pleased as well with her dance progress and complimented her over and over.

The other two trainees also arrived together. Carl Young escorted a sweet Annalea Montgomery in through the door. Annalea had soft light brown eyes on a face with no make-up and equally soft brown hair pulled back by a schoolgirl headband. She was a good seven inches shorter than the almost six foot Carl. Her dated shirt style dress was belted with a woven piece and looped to hold the gathers of the patterned dress at her waist. The skirt was right at knee length and her shoes loafers with scuffed toes. She carried the shoe bag with her heavy character shoes in one hand and her well worn purse in the other. There was a round softness to her body as if it had not an ounce of muscle tone – squishy flesh on a somewhat lean body. But Carl Young was gazing at her as if she were Miss America. His pale face and light hair barely moved from its attentive stare at her shy expression.

Megan groaned. Oh, no. Not another budding romance. She could hardly take another one! She reminded herself she would have to have the grooming speech with the lovely Annalea. Dress appropriately in a businesslike manner and always, always wear make-up. Maybe Amanda could do a little makeover on this new trainee.

Megan leaned back in her chair and considered the past few weeks of love and romance here in the studio. First, there was Edward and Amanda's wedding. Yes, Edward had been selfish and inconsiderate and clearly foolish in his choices regarding his marriage and his fidelity, but the two were somehow a good match and very much in love. Too bad it had ended in divorce and death. It was a sorry state to be sure.

Then there was Jim Peterson and Annie St. Germaine. Another wedding between two who shared the same political views, religious experiences, and moral standards. How could it get any better than this couple? Yet, there were secrets. Megan didn't know all of the secrets, but those she experienced so far were not little white lies – they were big huge earth shattering surprises. Yes, there was something there that wasn't quite in line with truth. Some day Megan hoped she would understand all the complicated mysteries of this relationship.

Gigi and Barney Taft – now that was one strange couple! There was no love in this relationship. Only convenience. Barney had someone to push his wheel chair and accompany him on social engagements. Gigi had money and social status and money again. It was an arrangement that seemed to suit the two parties involved, but it was sadly not a love match.

So then there was Carson and KC. Another odd couple if they were even a couple. They spent more and more of their time and energy together. It seemed mostly to be platonic, but who knew what it was? Megan assumed they didn't even know so how could anyone else know. They were simply together, come what may.

Paddy and Stephanie? A romantic duo, that was for sure. Their eyes barely left each other's, and they seemed to share a commitment for dance and spending time together. Would they make it? Probably the best bet of any of the couples Megan had considered so far. Yes, they might just be the ones to have it all – love, career, dance, and each other. It might work. Only time would tell.

Now Carl Young and Annalea Montgomery? They seemed to be another odd couple. Annalea was a small town girl who was shy and quiet and very vulnerable. Carl? Megan hadn't quite decided who Carl Young was yet. Was he the man for such a woman as Annalea or was he a wolf in sheep's clothing?

As Megan was considering the impact love and marriage had played in the studio, Chandler Dane was arriving in New Orleans. He pulled a carry-on bag from the overhead compartment and descended the ramp to the airport. He didn't need to pick up a suitcase as he had traveled as light as possible hoping to only stay a few days. He fished out a piece of paper from his bag and carefully studied the names and addresses he had listed. First, he would need to check into his hotel. Or rather motel. Or rather flea trap. It was a cramped little room near the airport that proved to be very cheap – or as he liked to refer to it - inexpensive. He would have to use this description for his one of his comedy routines. It would trigger memories for many in his audience he was certain. He double checked to make sure the sheets and towels were clean and fresh. They smelled a bit musty but appeared to be OK. Then he pulled out a map of the city from his bag and began to trace the route he would have to take to reach the other destinations on his list. His itinerary was quite clear.

His next stop would be at the dance studio. It was the one Ashley Dobbs had been employed as a teacher when Edward had banished her from the Minneapolis studio. It was suppose to be the largest in the United States associated with the national group of studios affiliated with Edward's studio. Chandler was actually looking forward to seeing the place.

When he opened the door to his motel room, the hot summer air hit him squarely in the face. It was humid and uncomfortable. He found a taxi stand in the front of the motel with a vehicle parked and a driver leaning against the hood reading a newspaper. Chandler hopped in the taxi and got to the studio a few moments later. It was in the late afternoon. Most studios were busy in the evenings and rather slow during the day, but this studio was quite different. The building itself was a historical brick building with three stories and lots of vines climbing up the face of the front and winding around the wrought iron windows. Chandler paid the cabby and grabbing his bag, stood directly in front of the studio to stare. People were wandering in and out carrying dance bags and chatting. It appeared to be the social center of the neighborhood. He was impressed.

He followed an elderly couple in the front door and waited for the waft of cool air to slap his face. It felt heavenly. Music floated down the stairway. It seemed all three floors were occupied by the dance studio. A charming young lady greeted him at the front desk – an ornate structure from a time gone by. It was a breathtaking piece that would have impressed him if he were an antique dealer and not a comedian. But he appreciated its charm. He appreciated the charm of the receptionist much more, however. She had a cheerful smile, fluttering eyelashes, and a delightful accent.

"Hello, y'all," she drawled in a southern style that took his breath away. He wanted to be smart with a quick comeback but he just couldn't. He would simply try to be charming instead.

Leaning on the top of the desk, he introduced himself. "I'm Chandler Dane, a teacher from the Minneapolis dance studio owned by Edward Garrett." He extended his hand expecting a return hand, but the woman simply sat and stared at him with a grin on her face and a toss of her honey colored hair.

"And how can I help, y'all?" she asked with a cheery expression that made him realize this was her normal greeting, and he was nothing special to her. He was just another customer.

"Do you, or rather did you have a teacher by the name of Ashley Dobbs?" He tried to lean over and give her a sly wink.

"Ashley? Miss Dobbs? Well, yes we do." She turned to the wall at her back and flipped her hand toward a photo of the lovely Miss Dobbs in a posed portrait. Yes, there across the back of the reception desk were rows and rows of smiling staff photos. He didn't even want to count them all there were so many. Miss Dobbs' face was planted squarely in the second row above the photos of several seasoned veteran faces. She posed with a glance over a bare shoulder and a tilt of her head. Her eyes glowed and her even teeth showing pearly between bright parted lips. Her hair curled softly around her oval face and careened down her back. She was a vision.

"And just how many teachers do you have in this studio?" he asked letting his eyes scan the other faces pictured.

"Oh, today? Well, I'd guess we have about sixty on the staff right now. No, maybe seventy. We just graduated a new training class last Friday." She smiled back at him and tilted her head to the side for the next question.

"Do you…would you know where she is right now? Miss Dobbs, I mean." Chandler decided the best approach would be to be uninformed and ignorant about Ashley's situation. He might get what he needed if he appeared not to know anything at all.

"Well, I do believe Miss Dobbs is in the hospital. Why, yes she is." She looked down at her schedule as if it would tell her the answer to his question, which of course it didn't. He had already peeked over the top of the desk to note there were only names and times listed on that sheet and no information about a Miss Ashley Dobbs.

"Would you know what hospital that would be?" he waited anticipating the answer.

191

"Queen of Mercy. Yes, I do believe it is the Queen hospital they sent her to. It is quite close by. Just a few blocks actually," she seemed to be trying to get rid of him now. He noticed a line forming behind him with about three impatient people waiting to check in with this lovely Southern belle.

"You wouldn't mind if I just looked at the studio spaces, would you? Our studio just doesn't compare to what you have here." She waved him off with a go ahead nod, and he heard her greet the next person cheerfully with "Hello y'all!"

Chandler started up the stairs to take a look at the top floor first. The third floor was a massive dance floor. It was all open and filled with dancers in for their lessons. The music quickly changed from one song to the next. First, a Waltz played and then a Tango. No one seemed to notice the type of music playing. They just danced to the beat of the song. A few tables were shoved into the corners, but mostly the people in this area were dancing. The stained glassed windows surrounding the peaked alcoves were lovely and impressive. The dancers seemed oblivious to the breathtaking room. They must all be quite used to it by now as everyone else seemed to be completely focused on dancing and not in the beauty of the sunlight filtering through these magnificent stained glass windows and across the glistening wooden dance floor. But Chandler was gawking at the high ceilings and stunning window. Pressing himself into the wall so as to avoid any circling dancers, he gazed up mouth gaping. This truly was a stunning ballroom.

He moved down the staircase to the second floor. There were two smaller ballrooms – each larger than the Minneapolis studio's main floor. They were not quite as amazing. The windows were simple and less ornate that the third floor. Nonetheless, he let his jaw drop in amazement. These two ballrooms were also filled with students and teachers. He didn't want to disturb the busy receptionist who was helping another student and a small line was still in place waiting. He simply nodded toward her and peeked down the hallway to see the office doors in lines down the narrow carpeted aisle. He nodded to himself and then left the studio to trot down the few blocks to the hospital.

This would be a bit trickier. He needed a story to get some info from the hospital about Ashley Dobbs. His mind churned.

Looking haggard and carrying his bag in front of him, he pretended to wipe the sweat from his forehead as he approached the information desk. It certainly was not a stretch as the sweat was actually pouring down his face in reality from the humid heat of the day. He asked about one of their patients, Ashley Dobbs and was told she was no longer at this hospital. He quickly looked perplexed and disturbed, explaining he had come all the way from her home town of Minneapolis to have her sign some very important papers. He absolutely needed to see her as soon as possible. Plopping his bag on the top of the desk, he began to pace nervously back and forth to give the impression of great urgency. The receptionist politely tried to look through records to give him any information about her location. Then informed him Miss Dobbs had been transferred to Mercy Hospital. When he asked what date the move had been made, the receptionist curtly told him the date – the day after Edward Garrett's murder.

Chandler nodded his head. It was what he had expected. Then before getting directions to Mercy Hospital, he asked if Miss Dobbs' physician was available for him to talk with. He decided the more information, the better. The receptionist directed him to the second floor and promptly went back to her phone which was now ringing.

The hospital halls felt stark and pale. He had expected more people to be moving around but it was indeed quite still. He found a nurse who directed him to a man in blue scrubs staring at a clip board. Chandler introduced himself as a friend and co-worker of Ashley Dobbs sent to collect some signatures for an important legal document. The man simply peered over his wire rimmed glasses and stared – waiting for more.

"Could you tell me why Miss Dobbs was transferred to Mercy Hospital?" Chandler pulled up to his full height and tried to look rather official.

"We simply didn't have the right facilities to care for Miss Dobbs. So her mother and our staff made a decision to move her to a facility that could." He was crisp and to the point not really giving away any details or information that wasn't known already.

"So you sent her in an ambulance to Mercy?" Chandler frowned looking to the paper in his hand as if consulting his own notes.

"Oh, no." The doctor frowned right back shaking his head firmly. "Her mother transported her over to the hospital, and they called to confirm her admittance."

"They?" Chandler probed.

"The Mercy Hospital staff, of course." Now he was getting quite irritated at all the questions and simply turned to move on his way.

Now Chandler was getting quite excited. This was an interesting development. Laura Dobbs herself transported lovely Ashley to the next hospital. He could hardly wait to get to Mercy. Racing out of the drab hospital, he grabbed a taxi and headed across town to the older run down hospital that stretched across two full blocks.

By now he was getting quite good at this routine. He scurried in with his bag and explained he must see a patient, Ashley Dobbs to get signatures for some very important legal documents, and the receptionist directed him to the third floor west wing. This time the hospital seemed teaming with people. People waiting, walking, hobbling, and resting. Some were even leaning along the walls or rather holding onto the walls for support.

Chandler tried to maneuver around those blocking the passage ways and took the elevator to the third floor. He tried to follow the signs that directed him to the west wing, and the crowds seemed to diminish quite a bit on this floor of the hospital.

The nurse at this station was harried and when asked about Ashley Dobbs waved him toward one of the rooms as she continued a heated conversation with an angry person on the other end of the phone. Chandler slipped on by and entered the room indicated. There was a single bed and a person huddled in fetal position under a thin white sheet. He could see her brown hair streaming away from the edges of the linens. He moved closer and called Ashley's name softly. No response. He called out again moving even closer, but there was no movement from the person in the bed. Finally, he pulled back the sheet for a quick look. This certainly wasn't Ashley Dobbs. He knew Ashley's face from the pictures Megan had shown him of the parade – that retched first routine she shared with her partner Edward Garrett. Pulling the few photos Megan had given him before his trip, Chandler gazed at one glossy print and matched the features. The woman lying in this hospital bed was definitely Claire Benson. She appeared to be either very ill or drugged, and he bet on the drugging after glancing at her chart clipped to the foot of her bed. The medications listed seemed a mile long.

He pulled out his cell phone and quickly called Megan Meeker at the studio. "We've got a problem," he began. Quickly he explained who he had found in Mercy

Hospital. Then he suggested she call the Minneapolis police to intercede for them and contact the New Orleans police department.

Chandler sat quietly in the chair next to Claire's bed and waited. No one checked on her and no one noticed him – that is until the police arrived. Then the questions began to fly. Who had admitted this patient and why was she in this state? What did they believe to be her condition? After the pointing of fingers from all sides, the police agreed to let Chandler Dane and a police woman escort the still very drugged Claire Benson back to Minneapolis. Maybe in a few hours or even days, there would be some answers for this very puzzling predicament, but for now the missing woman had been found alive and hopefully well. Time would tell.

Megan Meeker received several phone calls – Chandler, the New Orleans police, and the Minneapolis police – all explaining parts of the story as they understood it. Laura Dobbs had taken Ashley – the real Ashley – out of Queens Hospital, then substituted Claire for Ashley when admitting her to Mercy. The staff at Mercy had been told "Ashley" needed heavy sedation for her problems with depression, and they had complied with Laura's requests. Indeed, during one episode when "Ashley" had insisted she was not really Ashley Dobbs, the staff believed she was experiencing hallucinations. They had actually increased her dosage to avoid any further altercations with the young woman.

Chandler walked from the airplane accompanied by a half smiling Claire who was supported on one side by Chandler and the other side by a uniformed officer. Megan, Mary, and Claire's mother had rushed to greet the group with such joy that Claire almost collapsed again but Chandler stayed steady and supported her tiny thin body successfully as everyone wrapped arms around her neck and shoulders. Tears ran down her mother's cheeks – clearly a reconciliation was in the future for the two.

Claire was weak, but able to fill in a few details for the police. Laura Dobbs had approached her in the street outside Orchestra Hall just prior to the wedding show. She was in a wheelchair and asked Claire if she could wheel her in for the show. Claire knew Ashley had mentioned her mother's health issues so of course Clair had eagerly agreed to help the poor woman. But when they had entered the building and moved around toward the stage area where Laura claimed to have a meeting with someone, Laura asked for help with her shoes. Claire had walked around the wheelchair and knelt to deal with the shoe problem and didn't remember anything after that. Either Claire had been hit in the head or drugged, but she had no memory of Edward Garrett and his death, the plane ride to New Orleans or the admittance to the hospital. In fact, she was quite shocked to hear of Edward's murder from Chandler when they were returning from New Orleans, and he had filled her in on some of what she had missed. There were times during her hospital stay when she had tried to communicate with the staff as to who she was, but she was drugged most of the time and left in a state of bewilderment

198

as to where she was and why she was there. It had all be quite confusing for her. She was totally unaware as to the number of days and weeks she was away. Time had stood still.

Now the question was where was the real Ashley Dobbs? The police had immediately gone to the apartment shared at one time by Ashley and her mother Laura, but no one was there. They had left several days earlier according to neighbors. The rooms were cluttered with trash and unusable junk indicating they had left in a hurry.

"How did Laura Dobbs manage this charade?" Megan demanded of Chandler when they finally settled in Edward's old office for a review of his trip to New Orleans. "And does this mean Laura is indeed responsible for Edward's murder?"

"I knew you would ask that very thing, so I went to the airport myself and discovered Laura Dobbs did indeed fly to New Orleans the day before Edward's death, but she returned on a different flight under a different name – Laura Hamilton. Then she returned to New Orleans with her 'daughter' in a wheel chair on the day Edward died." Chandler had done lots of leg work. Megan was impressed. "The airline attendant remembered her quite specifically because of the daughter in the wheel chair. The daughter was quite unresponsive and seemed to be very ill. What do you make of that?"

"The only thing I know is we've found out what happened to Claire Benson. She must have been the daughter in the wheel chair. But why? Why take Claire to New Orleans?" Megan twisted her face into a contorted thought mode.

"Obviously to free the real Ashley from her hospital stay," Chandler stated smugly.

Megan shook her head. "She could easily have taken Ashley out of the hospital and home to Minneapolis without replacing her with Claire. After all Ashley wasn't a prisoner. She was free to go whenever she pleased." Megan stretched her arms out as if asking the heavens for help to solve this dilemma.

"Well, it would have given them both an alibi for the murder, and it would have given the impression Claire was indeed the murderer. That must be it." Chandler shook his head. It seemed to make sense. "But now what? Where are they now and what will they do next?"

"With the plan discovered on the New Orleans end, it will be dangerous for all of us. There could easily be more to the plot than just murdering Edward Garrett. Who would they go after next?" The two pondered this new question.

"If your story is correct about the affair and all, I'd say Amanda Garrett might be the next target. If they are looking for the person who made Ashley Dobbs suffer, it would be first and foremost Edward and second, Amanda. She discovered and broke up the affair after all." Chandler was becoming very good at moving beyond the obvious. He was thinking outside of the box.

Megan decided to speak with Amanda Garrett one on one. This was not a matter to discuss over the phone. So bright and early the next morning, she headed to the studio where Amanda would be conducting her usual morning exercise class. There would certainly be time for an in depth conversation with the lovely Amanda Garrett after her class.

Indeed the studio was already busy. Amanda was in the front of the group in her usual torn dance togs – pale pink tights with toes and heels cut out jaggedly with a scissors, clinging leotard covered by a loose fitting short cropped sweatshirt that hung off her shoulders. Her bare feet spread into a second position in front of the floor to ceiling mirrors kept her body balanced as she let her curly topped head fling from side to side. The music pounded with a steady beat as the models behind her imitated their leader in movement. The group had grown since Edward's death. There were about fifteen – both men and women. Most of the group dressed in stylish colorful exercise wear but a few were dressed down like Amanda. Megan recognized one male model who had attended these groups for a number of years standing in the back row. He wore an old fashioned sleeveless white t-shirt – the kind Marlon Brando wore in some of the old 50's movies when he was a young heart throb. His pants were baggy and pleated for ease of movement. Megan had never been attracted to his handsome appearance as his personality was lacking any appeal. He spent most of his time admiring himself in the mirror and any conversation always lead to a discussion of his "wonderfulness". It was gagging at times.

Megan motioned to Amanda. As they took a quick break between exercises, Megan asked if Amanda had a few moments to talk after the session was finished. "It's about Ashley Dobbs," Megan explained briefly. Amanda frowned but nodded her agreement.

The group continued their exercises to a newer song Megan recognized from the radio. Edward had always picked out the newest most edgy music to exercise to, and evidently Amanda was trying to continue that trend. She flung her head from side to side and let her hips sway. Megan checked over her bookings for the day and gazed across the desk to the mirror to watch the group – some successfully and some not even close to matching their leader's dance moves. What was Megan going to say to the lovely Amanda? And where could Laura and Ashley Dobbs be? Probably out of the country. That was Megan's guess. The police would no doubt try to discover a path for the two after Laura's journey back home from New Orleans. Neighbors were not particularly helpful as the two seemed to keep a low profile never making friendships with those living around them. And was Edward's murder due to anger? Anger because he dropped the unstable Ashley Dobbs after their quick but volatile affair? Others were known to have committed murder for less. It seemed very possible.

Amanda Garrett wandered off the floor in conversation with two beautiful young women who were giggling and cheerfully thanking her for the exercise opportunity. Amanda's hollowed cheeks and thin pressed lips were somber as she faced Megan Meeker seated behind the front desk. The others in the group were pulling on oversized tops and grabbing large shoulder bags stuffed with who knows what. Megan waited glancing at the group as they left, then stood and circled the desk.

"Can we go into Edward's office? It's rather important," Megan motioned toward the door.

She let Amanda sit behind the desk, and Megan sat in front of the desk. Amanda had a slight grin on her face as she allowed herself to playfully twirl a few times in the large overstuffed chair like a child on a merry-go-round. Then she settled in and waited for Megan to tell her whatever news she had – most likely about Edward's death.

"We've found Claire Benson," Megan began.

Amanda's eyebrows raised slightly, and she waited for the next part of the conversation to unfold. Possibly she still imagined Claire was responsible for Edward's death.

"Laura Dobbs kidnapped her from the Wedding Show on the day of Edward's murder and flew with her down to New Orleans." Megan waited to see Amanda's reaction which was one of utter surprise before continuing. It seemed quite genuine. "We, or rather Chandler Dane –

you remember dear Chandler? Found her in a hospital drugged and admitted as 'Ashley Dobbs'."

At this Amanda's eyes widened and her mouth rounded into a surprised "Oh, my!" Now Megan could see Amanda's brain churning with the new information.

"Claire is fine now that she is home, but we don't know where Laura and Ashley are at the present time," Megan leaned forward and rested her elbows on the edge of the large desk gazing steadily into Amanda's eyes.

"Do you think Laura Dobbs was responsible for Edward's murder?" Amanda's face was now an ashen white as she chewed on her lower lip. "This is quite disturbing," she murmured as she pondered the implications of this news.

"I'm sure the police are looking at the two as possible suspects. Do you know where they might be?" Megan could see the wheels of Amanda's mind churning in thought.

"No." She hesitated. "No, I can't think of any place they might be."

"Amanda," Megan added slowly. "I'm worried Edward's death might not be the end of this."

"What do you mean by that?" Amanda sat back in the chair letting it lean a bit and gripped the armrests.

"There has to be a reason they kidnapped Claire and put her in Ashley's place. Maybe to give themselves an alibi. Maybe it was something else. But there seems to be more to this than just Edward's murder, and it makes me nervous." Megan began to ponder. "It's got to be more than just revenge."

"Revenge? You think it was for revenge?" Amanda's face twisted and her voice became more forceful. "Then why not me and not Edward? If I were the victim, then Edward would be free to have a relationship with Ashley and all would be good as gold again. Right?"

"That's right!" Megan agreed nodding slowly. It made more sense to get rid of Amanda. Why didn't they?

"Maybe it wasn't revenge at all," Amanda's mouth pressed into a severe line across her face.

"Maybe it was something else. But whatever the reason, I wanted to warn you to be very careful. Very careful." Megan repeated her warning just to be sure it was registering with Amanda the importance of this latest development.

Amanda and Megan both rose from their seats and moved into the reception area. There was a new electricity in the air that made Megan feel uncomfortable. Amanda grabbed her bag and left immediately with a slight stoop to her shoulders. Megan sensed there was something on Amanda's mind – something she wasn't sharing.

As Amanda exited the door, a couple proceeded in through the door. The woman was tall and large boned but with a stunning beauty – very Nordic even for Minnesota. Her hair was a pale blond with a short fluffy cut and her face sported a square jaw and a glowing smile. She wore a long straight cut dress that emphasized her flat stomach and well toned upper body. Even wearing flat sandals, she was about two inches taller than her husband who followed her through the door with a puppy dog expression of obedience. He had a clean cut sandy head of hair with a soft handsome face. He looked to be a perfect preppy college student and probably was about that very age – early twenties. His polo shirt and khaki pants were casual yet well pressed. But his shoulders slouched slightly as he reluctantly followed his energetic wife through the door.

The woman stuck out her hand and introduced herself and then her husband. "Hello. I'm Kelly Clark Johns," and turning to her following husband announced "and this is my husband James Johns." He nodded his head ever so slightly and smiled as if this were about the last place on earth he wanted to be standing.

Continuing, Mrs. Johns asked about dance lessons. "I'm wondering if we could come in for a few lessons. Dancing has always been one of my dreams." She smiled brightly as James Johns stifled a yawn behind her back.

Megan Meeker smiled back at the woman and pulling out a studio business card selected a time the next day for a lesson with Paddy O'Grady. Mrs. Johns gazed at the card with a dreamy stare, then let her lips curl into an pleasant smile. Mr. Johns dug his hands into his pants pockets and waited patiently as Megan imagined he did quite often. The two turned to leave just as Carl Young and Annalea entered together. Carl nodded an acknowledgement and let his head follow the pair out the door. He stared until they reentered the elevator and the door slid closed.

Carl Young sauntered up to the front desk where Megan was studying her schedule for the day as Annalea plopped onto one of the chairs in the reception area to change her shoes. She slipped out of a pair of comfortable flats into her heavy clunky character shoes playing a few minutes with the complicated straps.

"We'd like to make an announcement," Carl declared with a sarcastic confidence. Megan looked up and waited. "We are engaged." Carl smiled and leaned on the top of the reception desk counter eyes narrowed waiting for a reaction. Annalea quietly kept her head bowed.

"Well, now. That is quite an announcement!" Megan sat back in her chair and remained expressionless. Too many things had happened recently for this to be a shock. "You haven't known each other all that long...". She cocked her head waiting for an explanation.

Carl placed his hands on the top of the desk and flatly answered back, "No, but when you know someone is right for you, you jump on it. And that's that," he declared.

"Well, best of luck," Megan turned her eyes back to her paperwork. Carl Young glared at her with frustration. Obviously he thought the news would create some kind of stir. He was almost angry that it was taken so lightly. He pulled up to his full height and snorted loudly.

"And we are getting married this weekend," he continued. This time both Megan and Annalea lifted their heads to stare. Finally, something got their attention he seemed to think as his faced turned to a look of satisfaction.

"Carl, dear...", Annalea's voice began to drone thin from behind him. His head spun with a look that warned her against saying anything else, and she shrunk back shoulders hunched snapping her mouth closed and tightly pressed together.

"You are all invited to a small reception at the Clarion," he lifted his nose in the air and continued defiantly as he named the elegant hotel down the block. At this Annalea coughed uncontrollably. Once again he turned his head to glare.

"Oh, Paddy," Megan looked right past Carl to Paddy O'Grady as he escorted Stephanie in through the front door. "I booked a new couple with you for tomorrow. Check the schedule for the time, please." Megan began to tap her pencil eraser on the schedule.

All four people in front of the desk looked from face to face as if startled by something but didn't know what it was. So Megan explained carefully as she

208

continued to look down at the schedule in front of her. "Well, Carl and Annalea are engaged and getting married this weekend, and Mr. O'Grady has a new couple to teach coming in tomorrow." At this Paddy lifted an eyebrow, and Stephanie in turn lifted her eyebrow as well making them look like a matched set of bookends.

"Married? Well, congratulations man!" Paddy boomed with his usual sonic voice and extended a hand to shake toward Carl Young who was by now strutting like a peacock with a smirk on his pasty bland face. "And to you, too," Paddy twirled and stretched his arms wide for a hug from Annalea who was still mumbling something about her parents being unable to attend something quite so soon. "Hey," Paddy continued, "Steph and I have talked about that possibility as well. Not quite so soon…". He turned toward Stephanie who this time raised both eyebrows as if to say "not another word!"

After the four retreated to the teachers' office, Megan leaned back in her chair to once again ponder love. She shook her head as she thought about Carl Young and the innocent passive Annalea. How would this marriage fare? She wasn't sure, but didn't have high hopes for success. Too soon, too soon. Yes, she had heard of couples who met and married within a few days of their first encounter then managing to have fifty years of wedded bliss, but Carl and Annalea didn't quite seem to be so well matched as those who professed these successes.

The news was a shocker indeed for the rest of the staff. Carson was furious. Megan could tell because he didn't say one word about it. When Carson didn't speak, it meant he was displeased and didn't want to talk about it. Sydney simply shook her head and ignored the ranting and arrogant Carl who bantered on and on about the whole thing for days until the event was thrust upon everyone. KC didn't seem interested in the slightest. She hadn't bonded with either Carl or Annalea, so just shrugged off any mention of the upcoming wedding. Would anyone actually attend the reception? Megan felt an obligation and talked Chandler Dane into accompanying her. He was reluctant but finally agreed. "Weddings aren't my thing," he whined but finally gave in when she mentioned the possibility of free food.

Carl Young had spoken too soon, as seemed to be his usual trait. The reception was held after a civil ceremony and was at the Clarion but in a rented room that he and Annalea would use for their one night honeymoon. It was actually a perfect size for the six or so people who did attend. Poor Chandler found the offer of food was a bit over exaggerated and was simply a bowl of chips and an opened plastic vat of onion dip. There was, however, champagne flowing freely. But after a glass each, both Megan and Chandler decided to head down to the hotel bar for a nightcap and an order of hot onion rings. Real food.

"I'm afraid that marriage will be another sham," Megan predicted sipping her glass of wine.

"Another sham?" Chandler asked. "Did I miss one?"

"Didn't you ever meet Barney Taft and his not so wifely wife Gigi?" Megan moaned. When Chandler shook his head, Megan explained about their arrangement. "She wheels him around and acts as a companion in exchange for money. It's a business proposition. Works but seems sad." Megan shook her head thinking about the delightful Barney Taft. She hadn't wanted to, but she had liked the man immensely. In her heart she wanted Barney to be loved for who he was – loved and happy. Maybe he was happy. Who was she to judge? Now Carl and Annalea was another story. Annalea had looked sweet and innocent in a long sleeved cotton white dress she probably had bought off the rack in a discount store earlier this week. It looked simple and plain but new. She had worn her hair down with big looping curls she had done herself with a curling iron. A tiny bobby pin held back the hair from her face. She had put on a bit of pink blush on her cheeks and a touch of lip gloss. Carl wore a black suit with a white shirt and black bow tie. Plain but groom-like. Annalea seemed to be taking in deep breathes of air throughout the reception and had even complained about feeling a bit faint during the ceremony. None of her family was able to attend. The timing was just too soon for any of them to cancel already made plans. She had mentioned she hoped they could repeat the ceremony later for her family when the time was convenient. Carl had frowned at that suggestion but patted her patronizingly on the shoulder as she explained the plan to those who had attended. Megan didn't think it would ever actually happen but she hoped for Annalea's sake that Carl would consider the possibility.

True to form, Paddy and Stephanie came in on Monday with a new stunning diamond on Stephanie's finger. Immediately Megan's thought was "Monkey see, monkey do!" but then she dismissed that thought and tried to look at the whole thing in a better more positive light. "Good for you," she had said to the pair when Paddy made the announcement – a little more cheerily than Carl had the previous week. The staff clapped politely at the news.

"And when is the big day?" Carson had asked peering down his nose at the delighted Paddy O'Grady.

"Oh, not for quite a while. We want to take our time with all the arrangements," Paddy declared sensibly in his booming voice. Stephanie sat smiling in a business-like suit of knotty tweed with her hair pulled back into a severe bun and just the right amount of make-up to look completely professional. Her long legs crossed flipping a black pump up and down casually.

Megan suspected the two made this announcement today because Carl and Annalea had taken the day off for their honeymoon that would last all of two days. It was easier to talk about their event with the newlyweds gone. Megan sighed in relief at their foresight. Carl Young would have made the whole announcement one of rivalry. It would have been an ugly scene.

Later that day Kelly Clark Johns with her husband at her heels arrived for a second lesson with Paddy O'Grady. She looked lovely in a crisp short dress with a red rose patterned fabric and a pearl choker. She wore a pair of summer white flats and flipped off a pair of expensive sunglasses.

"Ready for your lesson?" Paddy's voice boomed as he sharply walked in a brisk clip toward the couple carrying a program in hand.

"Well, I was wondering actually if I could speak to your manager when the lesson concludes," Kelly ventured as she peered down her nose and batted her long lashes at Paddy who took no notice but waved to Megan at the desk.

"Could we arrange a meeting with you after the lesson?" he called out.

"Actually, I would like to speak with you privately," Kelly clarified in a soft tone of voice that contrasted with Paddy's and smiled with a slightly tilted Cheshire grin.

"Certainly," Megan nodded. Hmmm. I wonder what this could be about? She made a point to watch the lesson carefully so as to comment with a more educated understanding of the couple's dance ability. Kelly Clark Johns was rather good. She seemed to pick up the patterns easily with only a quick demonstration. James Johns however, seemed content to move as little as possible. This irritated the lovely Kelly to no end. She spent the entire lesson stomping her foot and asking for a little cooperation from her sloth-like husband. Paddy O'Grady smiled endlessly trying to be patient but his temper was beginning to show a bit as he snapped at Kelly after one confrontation between husband and wife.

"Well, I can guess what this will be about," Megan complained to no one in particular. She looked over her schedule to find a suitable teacher to switch the couple's lessons. Sydney Monroe would be a good substitute but she only had one opening this week. Carson could take them if they could come in Wednesday afternoon.

Megan stood and moved around the desk when she saw the lesson was about to end. Checking her watch for time, she expected the next conversation to be from a complaining student asking for a new instructor. She never expected what was about to come.

Seated in front of Edward's former desk, Kelly Clark Johns looked pleasant enough. She scooted her chair closer for a more intimate conversation. Megan Meeker took a deep breath and waited for the wrath to begin.

"I would like to join your staff," Kelly Clark Johns announced with a pert tone to her voice.

"Excuse me?" Megan blinked her eyes and waited for an explanation.

"I think I could be a great asset to your studio. I would like to – well, frankly have your job. I want to close sales. I'm very good at it. I like the dancing, and although I am not at the level of your teachers presently, I feel I could learn quickly enough to understand the business of a dance studio." She sat back in her chair and watched

214

Megan Meekers' shocked face go from total surprise to confusion to thought.

"What exactly are you proposing?"

"I have always loved dancing. But I am a business woman at heart and experience and a very good one I might add. I am willing to come in as a closer to help really build the business you already have. I think I could really make a difference for you – and your partners. I believe you own this studio along with Mr. Hunter, Miss Monroe, and Miss Clark – no relation, by the way." She smiled as if she just made a humorous joke. "It's a common name," she added when she noticed Megan was not laughing. Kelly Clark Johns had clearly researched this studio prior to her arrival.

"Let me get this straight…you want a job? In management?" Megan stated the whole proposal simply.

"If you put it like that, yes." Kelly Clark Johns smiled in a most delighted manner that could only be described as "sunny". "I know most dance studios have a new student department and an advanced department. It seems to me you are doing double duty – triple duty if you count managing. I am willing to take over your new student department as a counselor and do all the sales thus freeing you to focus on the advanced department and the task of managing the entire operation." Yes, Kelly Clark Johns had done her homework. She knew what to say and what was needed. She sat back smugly and waited for the answer she expected – a resounding yes.

Megan Meeker paused. Her mind was churning rapidly. She wanted first to find out why this woman had made such a proposal and second, she wanted with all her might and strength to say "yes". But she knew she also had to do a bit of homework on her own. Nothing like this could be taken lightly. It had to be pondered and discussed and debated.

"I'll take your offer to our board," she snapped quickly before she could change her mind and accept too readily – to anxiously – to greedily.

"Fine," Kelly Clark Johns smiled and rose to leave. "I'll be back tomorrow when you open." She reached across the desk for a handshake. Smiled broadly and flounced out the door snapping up her husband who was wandering around the reception area and exited.

XV.

Gathering together the four executives on the ownership board, Megan presented Kelly Clark Johns' proposal. Their faces showed their shock and curiosity.

"Did she happened to mention money?" was Carson's first comment. His eyes narrowed suspiciously.

"Nope. Not a mention of the word."

"So what would be her motivation?" Sydney was tapping her fingers on the top of the table nervously.

Megan glared at her and whispered, "That tap, tap, tapping reminds me of Edward Garrett and his nervous habits in our staff meetings. Are you nervous by chance?"

"Well, whenever an offer looks too good, it makes me wonder. I guess you could say I'm a bit nervous. What do we know about this woman?" Sydney stopped her finger tapping and searched the faces of the others for answers.

"Why not ask Chandler to investigate and find some information for us before we make a decision? He seems to know how to do that sort of thing," KC spoke up for the first time, her eyebrows knit into a thick line across her forehead.

"Good point. Let's call him right away before she comes back tomorrow," Megan's eyes widened. She was not looking forward to another meeting with the woman so soon. They had to have a better idea of what and whom they were dealing with that was certain.

Chandler called back at the end of the evening. "Got to make this short and sweet," he started. "I go on stage in a few minutes. Kelly Clark Johns is from a very wealthy family. She has a degree in Business and is very good at what she does. She's been with several well-known firms and does a wonderful job – comes with glowing reviews. However, she gets bored easily and moves on quickly looking for adventure it seems. I guess you – or rather the studio is her latest playground. She seems to be very interested in the dance business. If you are worried about her trying to take over, I'd say you shouldn't worry.

She is just a moth flitting from one candle to another looking for new and better opportunities before moving on to something else. The studio is a kick for her. A new stomping grounds to see what she can do, that's all. Got to go!" And he hung up abruptly leaving Megan to ponder.

Hmmm. Megan relayed this information to the rest of the board. "It looks like we have nothing to lose!" KC spouted what the rest were thinking. "Negotiate a good pay schedule and don't let her take control of the situation."

Carson laughed, and Megan smugly leaned back in her chair imagining what it would be like to have a few free minutes a day. It might be quite a nice change after all. But when she got home, Megan did not sleep well. There was something not right about this whole situation. She couldn't put her finger on the problem. Chandler had given a concise report that seemed to present a favorable decision for Ms. Clark Johns joining the staff, but Megan still tossed and turned all night long.

Worn and worried, Megan got to the studio at about the same time Kelly Clark Johns sauntered up nursing a large latte from the corner coffee shop. Uncanny how she just happened to know when to arrive, thought Megan fishing for her key.

"You must have a sixth sense or something," Megan frowned as she slipped her key into the lock. Amanda and her models were exercising already but Amanda had decided to take the precaution of locking the door again after the last one arrived. Just for added peace of mind.

"You might say that," Kelly Clark Johns grinned. Her blond halo circled her head giving her an added glow in the early morning sunlight. She wore a navy business skirt with a small slit up the back, matching navy flats and an expensive knit top with a soft patterned stripe in navy, gold and magenta. Too appropriate, thought Megan. Businesslike but not too much.

The two sat once again in Edward's office. Kelly nursed her coffee as she stared at Megan trying to gain an insight into what her answer would be. The silence was broken by an abrupt change of music from the exercise class – one short blast before the volume was lowered to a more moderate tone.

"We've taken your offer into consideration," Megan began. There was silence. "And we've decided to take your offer. Yes, you will be our new student counselor." Megan's words hung in the air without a hint of excitement or congratulations. It was a simple statement of fact.

Kelly Clark John's mouth stretched into a knowing smile. "I had hoped you would say that. Thank you. You won't regret your decision. I can promise you that." She lowered her eyelids to stare into the swirling coffee cup she clutched on the desk top and let a slight grin cross her lips. Clearly, Kelly Clark Johns was not surprised by the announcement.

Megan suggested they go over their programs carefully before the rest of the staff arrived so Kelly would have an understanding of the business and how it worked on a daily basis. Pulling out the dance programs offered at the studio, Megan gave Kelly an explanation for each as if Kelly were a student ready to make a decision on a dance course. Kelly Clark Johns listened carefully and asked intelligent and insightful questions after each presentation. By the end of the hour, Megan was impressed with the knowledge Kelly would offer the studio. She was a well versed businesswoman. Megan recognized there was a lot Kelly could offer to this organization. Her experience was indeed vast.

At the daily staff meeting, Megan introduced Kelly to those who had never formally met her before. Then Kelly Clark Johns sat back and observed. She listened and watched the remainder of the meeting without so much as saying a word. Carl and Annalea were back from their "honeymoon" of two days. Carl's face turned a slight shade of pink when he learned of Paddy O'Grady's engagement to the lovely Stephanie Booker. However, rather than show a tinge of rivalry, he turned his attentions instead to the newest member of the staff, Kelly Clark Johns. He would turn and smile sweetly at her whenever a remark was made about his schedule for the day or an upcoming event. Was it to make Annalea jealous? Had they had their first disagreement already, and he needed to make a point?

After the meeting, Kelly pulled Megan aside for a request. "I'd like my darling James to come in for lessons. Could we arrange something?" She batted her eyelashes innocently.

"Actually, Annalea Montgomery er.. Young could use some practice teaching. We could assign James as her first student to see how she copes with a beginner." Megan began to ponder what they should call Annalea now that she was married. Continue with Montgomery or change it to "Young" and have people ask questions about the name change? She sighed at the complications in a business like this where one must be so careful not to reveal personal details to clients. She would have to discuss this situation with Annalea. Maybe a makeover would also be appropriate with her first student assignment. Megan grabbed the phone and made a quick call to Amanda Garrett.

"Amanda, would you be willing to do a make-up class for my new trainees? There are a few who could really use some help." Megan stared at Annalea practicing her dancing in the corner of the ballroom. She was such a sweet young thing but really needed a boost of confidence in her appearance. The mousy brown hair and pasty white complexion had to be transformed. And those dance shoes! God forbid she try to teach in those things. Megan shook her head and arranged for Amanda to stay after exercise class tomorrow for a session with the poor pitiful woman. She would invite Mary and Claire to join her. Maybe Stephanie would enjoy the pampering too. Not that she actually needed any help with her appearance. She always looked professional and crisp.

Claire and Mary were thrilled to have Amanda make them over. They gleefully danced around embracing each other, but Annalea seemed a bit skeptical. She appeared to be reluctant to improve her appearance in the slightest bit as if her world would collapse with any change. But when Megan mentioned she would be getting her first student tomorrow after the makeover, her attitude began to soften to the idea. She bit her lip nervously and seemed to ponder all of implications of her first teaching assignment and finally nodded her agreement to the plan.

The next day around eleven, the three of them sat at tables in the ballroom waiting for Amanda to finally finish her stretching and turn her attentions to them. Stephanie was working and could not make it, but Kelly Clark Johns was just sauntering in for an early work day when she spotted Amanda and her group. It was as if Kelly had never really noticed the tall, leggy woman before, or if she did, hadn't made any connections.

"Is that Amanda Kihn? The model?" she whispered to Megan stationed at the front desk as she continued to stare up and down at the agile model just finishing up her exercise routine.

Megan nodded not wishing to reveal Amanda's close association to the studio. She was very careful not to mention the murder to the studio's newest staff members and students. No need to mount any more gossip than there

222

already was. But Kelly seemed especially curious staring and asking questions that Megan tried her best to ignore.

Amanda cheerfully joined the women at the tables and began by having them all remove their make-up. Unfolding a large black case, she revealed tubes and colorful circles of eye shadows and lipsticks. She demonstrated how to apply the moisturizer and foundation, matching their skin tones to the perfect product. She applied a blush to Annalea's cheeks accentuating her cheekbones and contouring her face. Then she chose a complimentary lipstick and added a touch of gloss to give her lips shine. With a brush, she applied a soft brown shadow along Annalea's eyes just along the lash line on both the top and bottom. It was very subtle and soft but made her eyes pop. Amanda began to apply a peach tone to Annalea's eyelid and area under her brows to create an even palette. Then with a sweep of the brush, she added a darker brown along the lid line. With another larger brush, Amanda blended the colors together.

"Oh, Annalea, you look fabulous!" Mary gasped as she looked up from her own application process. Annalea leaned back and gazed into the mirror in front of her at the transformation. Her expression softened as she tilted her head slightly to view the changes.

"Let me work a little with your hair," Amanda pulled a tube of gel from her case and standing behind Annalea began to work her hands through the soft and shapeless hair. She generously squeezed the gel into her palms and began to play with the hair lifting it away from

Annalea's face. Moving around to the front of the woman, Amanda announced, "Now that looks much better!"

Amanda didn't stop there. With long flowing strides, she walked across the ballroom toward the costume closet and rummaging through snagged a pair of dance shoes. "Whenever a teacher leaves, they always seem to leave a pair of shoes or two. So we toss them into this closet. Now these should fit you nicely," Amanda pronounced handing Annalea a pair of strappy Latin sandals. The soft suede of the bottoms of the shoes were slightly worn but would be one hundred percent easier to do a Waltz in than the dreadful character shoes Annalea was used to wearing. The leather tops and straps would mold like a glove to her feet. Then Amanda searched the closet again for a circle skirt. "Here, try on this skirt. It will float a bit when you twirl." The black skirt was generic but fashionable and would match Annalea's beige top. With Annalea in the bathroom changing her clothes and slipping into the new dance shoes, Amanda continued to paw through the closet for a scarf or piece of fabric to give Annalea some color around her neck. Kelly Clark Johns watched curiously from the corner. Mary and Claire were finishing up their make-up application and "oohing" and "aahing" at the results.

Annalea returned with a swirl of the skirt and a strange new height with the heels giving her a straighter posture – a more confident appearance. Amanda twirled a soft scarf around her neck and tied it on the side playing with it so it circled nicely. "Very nice!" Amanda declared looking her up and down with a satisfied smile. Annalea scurried over to the mirror and surveyed herself. She had to agree. It was a welcome change. Pulling up to an erect posture, she looked very professional and contemporary. She was ready for her first lesson.

When Carl Young arrived at the studio, he gasped at the sight of his new wife. He stared, then he glared as if trying to let the new look register in his mind. Did he approve? He hadn't decided yet. His mouth clamped shut as he busied himself arranging the dance programs on the corner shelves.

James Johns was five minutes late for his lesson. Annalea waited anxiously at the front desk sighing occasionally anticipating failure. When he arrived, she seemed relieved but nervous. Kelly Clark Johns scampered up to him and gave him a quick peck on the cheek before he was led to the dance floor by Annalea.

"I wouldn't advise against kissing our students, even if he is your husband," Megan Meeker suggested crisply. "It's not professional."

Kelly Clark Johns flounced away to the back room with a sharp turn and an annoyed look on her face. She was not one to adhere to what appeared to be idiotic rules – she would soon discover why this one wasn't as ridiculous as it initially seemed to be. She would learn to be a more private person where personal information was concerned.

Amanda Garrett was gathering up her case and tote bag slowly slinging it over her shoulder. She approached the front desk and peered at Megan Meeker biting her lip as if hesitating to speak. Finally, she spoke. "I think I saw Ashley Dobbs."

Megan looked up with a fearful look in her eyes. "When? Where?" It was an odd statement for Amanda to make.

"I left a bit later than usual today because of the makeovers. I hadn't gotten all of my things together that I needed, so started for the studio after I normally do. I think I spotted her in front of my apartment building. I think she was watching for me. I surprised her. When I looked again she was gone. Disappeared."

"What will you do about this? Should I call the police for you?" Megan sat up straighter in her chair and reached for the phone.

"No. I can't do that to her. She is like my own child. I have an obligation to her," Amanda shook her head debating the possibilities in her own mind giving excuses for not acting.

"She may have killed your husband," Megan reminded firmly. "She may be a murderer."

"Not Ashley. Maybe her mother could do something like that, but not Ashley." Amanda lowered her chin and pursed her lips trying to convince herself of Ashley's innocence.

"But she betrayed you – her friend and mother figure. Is that someone to be trusted?" Megan's eyes narrowed to slits trying calmly to change Amanda's mind – to warn her of the dangers of being too trusting. Now was not the time to trust someone who had a history of poor judgment.

"Yes, this is true. It is true, but I must believe she means no harm to me." Amanda jutted her chin forward.

"If Ashley is nearby, so is her mother," Megan reminded. "Laura Dobbs must be close."

Amanda nodded her head slowly and shifting her case to the other shoulder readjusted her balance. "I'll take of this." She turned and walked out stiffly lugging her baggage – both physical and mental.

Annalea and James had an acceptable first lesson. James seemed to be more absorbed in what he was doing and attentive to his teacher than he had with Paddy O'Brien. Annalea was patient – sometimes hesitant – but more assured than she normally was. The shoes, the make-up and the hair seemed to act like a magic spell creating a new creature – a more confident being. She smiled as she escorted her student to the front desk to schedule the next lesson. James put his hand through his tasseled hair and allowed a slight smile to cross his lips. Annalea noticed and fingered her newly acquired scarf at her neck.

When James Johns walked out the door, Megan nodded toward Annalea. "Miss Montgomery, very nice lesson. You are becoming a competent teacher and an asset to the studio." Annalea smiled and walked steadily toward the teachers' office – her first time in that area of the studio.

Carl Young seemed to have mixed emotions that day. With no sign of being really proud of his wife, he arrogantly ignored her for the rest of the day pouting across the ballroom and flirting flagrantly with Kelly Clark Johns whenever possible. Annalea withdrew quietly until Claire and Mary approached her. "Don't you dare let that man treat you that way. You look wonderful, and you accomplished a great deal with your lesson today. He's just a jealous man who is trying to make you feel subservient to him. Don't let him do that! You are better than that." Claire whispered in her ear. "Yes, you are better than that," Mary agreed letting an angry look cross the ballroom to where Carl was chatting with Kelly Clark Johns.

XVI.

Megan was filling out student cards when the phone rang. It was the police informing her that Ashley Dobbs had been arrested. After hanging up the phone, she sat back in her chair. Amanda hadn't called the police after all to report the Ashley sighting. Instead it had been her father, Walter Kihn who had informed the police of Ashley's presence in the area. Amanda must have related her experience to her dad, and he had made the call to the police. She had passed on the dirty deed for her father to do rather than do it herself. Could anyone blame her? Not really. But now what? If Ashley had been here watching Amanda than surely Laura was as well. Megan hoped Amanda would be careful. She had the feeling Laura Dobbs was indeed more dangerous than Ashley.

Carson and KC left for the evening. KC cheerfully hooked her arm through Carson's and suggested a stop at the pub on the way home. Paddy and Stephanie laughed about a lesson Paddy had taught that evening as they huddled closely together and headed to the gym for a late night workout. Carl Young, hands in his pockets, sauntered out the door with Annalea back in her old loafers tripping along behind. Mary and Claire followed whispering, heads together ready to pounce on an unsuspecting Carl if he said anything negative to their newly acquired friend and confidant Annalea Montgomery Young. Sydney meandered up to the desk and encouraged Megan to put away her work for the evening and join her for a snack at the corner café. It sounded good.

Sydney and Megan sat in the small café at the corner with a large basket of chips and salsa and a couple of icy lemonades. Megan reported to Sydney about Ashley's arrest, explaining how Amanda had spotted the former teacher outside her apartment that morning.

"Do you think Ashley and Laura are responsible for Edward's death?" Sydney asked.

"It would appear so, wouldn't it?" Megan stated assuredly popping a chip laden with salsa into her mouth.

"Remember, things aren't always as they seem. Isn't that what you told me Maggie said to you? Things aren't always as they seem." Sydney looked around the small café. It was almost empty. "Do you want to stop in at the club on the way home? I'm not tired at all. I strangely feel like dancing tonight."

Megan settled back and realized she too was wide awake. "Sure."

They paid their bill and wandered down the street to the dance club a couple of blocks to the south. It was an art deco building plopped in the middle of a modern block. The stonework and copper accents were magnificent. It was late enough that the usual line to get in was no longer curved around the block. They slipped in easily and found a couple of stools in the balcony that circled above the dance floor. The music was pounding and loud. No possibility for conversation, so they simply watched the dramas that unfolded around them. Men in sleek pants and unbuttoned shirts trying to pick out women for drinks and conversation. The floor was filled with dancers weaving and spinning. Young and well dressed, the crowd was entertaining – like watching a soap opera. Megan and Sydney poked each other and giggled with each unfolding drama. A woman angry with her dance partner stalked off the dance floor leaving him with hands up in the air wondering – waiting for her return. A man was dancing affectionately with two women at the same time. Neither seem to care or react. They all simply danced and enjoyed the music.

Suddenly, Sydney poked Megan sharply in the ribs and nodded toward the back of the floor. Swaying seductively was Carl Young with Kelly Clark Johns. Megan looked shocked as they intertwined their arms and Kelly dropped her chin onto his shoulder. Where were Annalea and James? Where were their spouses? The floor turned dark as the music momentarily stopped. Silence. Then the next pounding beat of a new song and a flash of lights. The couple was no longer on the dance floor. They were swallowed up into the crowd. The night was done. Megan and Sydney both craned their necks to find the pair but they were nowhere to be seen.

The sun streamed in through the window as Megan slowly opened her eyes and peered at the clock by her pull out bed. Morning had come too soon. She wanted just a few more minutes – no hours - of sleep before getting ready for another day at the studio. Finally, flinging back her covers, she let her legs swing to the floor and hoped she had put the timer on the coffee pot last night. Sure enough. The aroma of brewing coffee lifted her spirits and energized her plight toward the bathroom. Another day. Another drama unfolding. She remembered the sighting of Kelly and Carl at the dance club last night, and it made her feel sick. What had happened to the word 'commitment'?" She felt as if she were living in a sappy movie. No one and nothing seemed to be as expected. If she and the studio staff had to go through another dramatic divorce, she didn't know what they would do. After all, the last one ended with a murder.

She managed to put on an adequate coat of make-up and slip into a striking emerald green dress and matching pumps. She remembered Amanda's little gel trick the day before and fluffed her hair nicely. Then after a small breakfast of coffee and cold cereal, she left to catch her bus.

Amanda and her models were in the middle of their exercise class with the music pounding in the background. Amanda looked lean and slim with her long legs spread, barefoot and wearing a short cropped knit top, she was swinging her body to the beat. Her curly hair was pulled up on top of her head and puffed out like a cotton ball. There were three beauties lined up in the first row behind her trying to imitate every move. The second row included two women and two men – all breathtakingly beautiful and the back row had one man lazily swinging from side to side without much effort. Megan smiled.

Sliding behind the reception desk, she began to prepare for the day. She checked the appointment schedule and made sure she was marked out for interviews and progress checks. She mentally made a note to take Kelly Clark John with her on all the new student procedures. It was time she began to learn her trade. She was a smart lady – at least sometimes. It should come easy for her. The front door bell rang.

Looking up, Megan saw Walter Kihn rush in. He glanced around wildly, his face ashen and his breathing heavy. Megan stood and leaned on the reception desk. "Can I help you Mr. Kihn?"

"Where's Amanda?" His head twisted from left to right and finally spotted his daughter lying on the floor. He rushed to her, kneeling down on the floor to feel her pulse.

"What are you doing, dad?" Amanda popped her head up with a frown. "What are you doing?"

"Are you all right?" Mr. Kihn was not a man who seemed to rattle easily. Megan cocked her head to watch this unusual display.

Suddenly from the back of the ballroom came a raspy voice. "Walter Kihn! Stand up. Let me see you."

Megan peered across the desk cautiously toward the mirrored walls and in the reflection spotted Laura Dobbs standing in the corner of the ballroom. She had entered through the back door and slipped through the little kitchenette by the parking lot pay booth. Edward Garrett always used that exit. Laura Dobbs certainly had been aware of this prior to today. She stood there erect and looking cool with a gun in her hands. It was pointed at Walter Kihn. It was pointed at Walter Kihn's head. She steadied herself by spreading her feet and locking her legs as she put both hands on the gun looking down the barrel at her victim.

"What is the matter with you?" Mr. Kihn snarled at the woman. The models and Amanda Garrett stood stone still - even the lazy man in the back row suddenly seemed alert. Their quick inhales sounded as surprised gasps as they realized this gun was indeed the real thing. "Let these innocent people go. They have nothing to do with this whole thing. Don't be stupid!" Walter Kihn waves his hand indicating the people now huddled behind him.

"Stupid? You think I'm stupid? You didn't think I was stupid when you called me …". Laura Dobbs began with a sputter – a jeering sputter.

"Shut up. Just let these nice people leave, would you?" Mr. Kihn waved his arms around at the class who stood with their mouths gaping opened.

"Sure, sure. All of them leave! You just don't want anyone to hear what really happened, do you? You," Laura pointed at Amanda Garrett, "stay." She waved the barrel of the gun loosely at the others motioning they should leave but pointed with her left hand at Amanda Garrett. The group scattered not even bothering with their duffle bags. They could hardly get out of the door fast enough. Amanda stood limply behind her father.

"Ok, missy. Listen to me. Your daddy here had my daughter Ashley arrested. Arrested! And they are bringing murder charges against her. Murder charges! She wasn't even in the state when your dear husband was killed. But your father had her arrested!" Laura Dobbs' face was now twisted in rage and her thin body was tensed as if a cat ready to pounce on a defenseless mouse. "She had nothing to do with that murder," Laura declared forcefully. "Nothing," she repeated.

"She is the reason my dear daughter and her husband split up because she is a slut. A sleazy little slut who has no respect or concern for anyone else but herself. No loyalty whatsoever!" Mr. Kihn's face was scrunched in anger as he pointed his finger at Laura Dobbs in reference to her daughter Ashley.

"Well, Mr. Walter Kihn," Laura Dobbs face softened and her voice became sing-songy sweet. She was smiling ready to spring new information on the man. "For your information that 'slut' as you call her is your own daughter!" Her voice had lowered to a raspy soft whisper.

Mr. Kihn's face went ashen. "What are you talking about?" He was spitting with anger.

"You, Mr. Kihn met a woman – a Miss Laura Hamilton – at a convention in Boston twenty – one years ago. That woman was me." Laura stuck her chest out and pointed to herself with her free hand as she once again waved her gun at Mr. Kihn's head. "And from that meeting a tiny little girl, one Ashley Marie Dobbs, was born. Or should I say, Ashley Marie Dobbs Kihn!" At this announcement, Amanda Garrett lowered herself to the ground, squatting and letting her head rest in her hands. Ashley Dobbs was her half sister.

Walter Kihn let his jaw drop. His mind began to churn. His tongue rewet his lips and licked across his upper row of teeth. He was carefully trying to study Laura Dobbs' face – trying to recognize her from his past. Clearly she was hazy. Did he remember her? Did he remember Boston? He shook his head slowly. Yes, he had visited Boston. But a Laura Hamilton? Maybe…

"And for your information, Miss Kihn or Mrs. Garrett," Laura directed her remarks toward Amanda. "Your dear daddy here, hired me to kill your husband. Ex-husband. Sorry about that." Laura again waved her gun as Amanda swooned and let out a low moan.

"He had it coming! He cheated on my daughter!" Walter Kihn snarled with a fierce shaking of his fist.

"With your other daughter!" At that Laura Dobbs laughed a hearty laugh letting her head tilt back. "What do you say now about respect and concern for others? How much respect did you have for your saintly wife to hook up with me? How many others were there? I'm quite certain I wasn't the only one. You are as guilty as your former son-in-law." She let a chuckle gurgle in her throat.

Amanda Garrett stood up. Her fists were clenched, and she moved from behind her father to his right. She stared at him and then back at Laura Dobbs. "Tell me again. My father hired you to kill Edward?" Her face hardened. She wanted the full story, and she wanted it now.

"Your dear daddy called me and asked me to kill Edward Garrett. He paid me quite handsomely I might add. When Ashley went into the hospital, I knew we had to do something. So when Walter called and made me an offer, I had to accept. So went to the wedding show early hoping to catch up with sweet little Claire Benson. I knew she had no family or friends in the area, so her disappearance wouldn't be questioned by those close to her. I had checked the bus schedule and knew when she would arrive. I rented a wheelchair and wheeled myself up to her. I knew she thought I was gravely ill, so the wheelchair would bring sympathy. I asked her to help wheel me in to a meeting scheduled with Edward. She was more than willing to help me out which I knew she would be. Ashley told me about all of the staff here. I knew Claire would be a sympathetic soul. When we got to the back stage, I drugged her with bit of ether on a cloth I had in a baggy under my blanket, spread her out on the floor and then ran for Edward's help. Of course he came with me and when he knelt down to help poor Claire, I hit him on the head. Then I strung him up with the curtain cord, put Claire in the wheelchair and wheeled her to the airport for the exchange at the hospital for Ashley. It was quite simple, really!" Laura was now bragging about her plan. "Walter paid us quite handsomely, but he still didn't know about Ashley." At this Laura's mouth twisted up at the corners into a wide grin. "She was my ace in case I needed extra protection from this weasel. I didn't trust him for one moment. He had left us high and dry after her birth. I moved here to Minneapolis with the intention of someday allowing

Ashley a relationship with her biological father. But when I initially sent a note about her existence, he cleverly ignored us not even asking such basic information as who were. He didn't even ask her name! He actually threatened to sue us and referred us to his lawyer for any further contact. We simply took the one time chunk of money the lawyer offered and disappeared waiting for the right time to reappear into his life. I knew there would be lots more money if we were patient. I was right. This is surely the right time."

Megan Meeker hiding behind the wall of stone and unseen by Laura Dobbs had called the police when the exercise class had scurried out the door. The noise made by the shuffling feet had allowed Megan a perfect opportunity for that one quick call. The police had an officer stationed in the small kitchen – the very one Laura Dobbs had entered. Another was at the front door waiting to storm the studio. Megan scrunched her body beneath the reception desk. Waiting.

"So what's your plan now?" Walter Kihn asked. "You going to kill me? Kill us?" He motioned toward his daughter Amanda.

"Oh no! I'm going to trade you two for my daughter. I'm going to get Ashley back from the police. So I'm just waiting for them to make their move. Yoohoo! Where are you?" Laura waved her gun around again. This was one clever woman.

The policeman from the kitchen entered, gun raised. Laura smiled. The policeman from the front door also entered. He side stepped around the edge of the wall until Laura could see him clearly.

Laura motioned for Walter and Amanda to move toward her. She told them to face away from her and put their hands up. "Officers, I want to make a trade," she announced with confidence oozing of her voice.

No one said anything. They waited for Laura Dobbs to continue. "I want to make a trade, gentlemen. I want to trade these very upstanding citizens for my daughter Ashley."

One policeman grabbed his phone from his belt and called headquarters. "She wants a trade..." he began. He listened intently.

"Tell them to bring Ashley here. To the studio." Laura demanded with a harsh rasp to her voice. She flung her hair out of her eyes and waited for their response.

"They are bringing her to the studio right now," he announced. "No need to get excited and do something foolish. We'll work with you. We don't want anyone hurt."

The time clicked on. Amanda Garrett stood sturdy with eyes down thinking. Ashley Dobbs was her sister. Did Ashley know? Had she known all along? Was it planned? The friendship. The affair. Had she been a part of the plan?

Walter Kihn rounded his shoulders. His daughter now knew about his indiscretions. His affairs. His plan to kill Edward. Not only did Amanda know, but these law enforcement officers also knew. He was done. His reputation shot.

Suddenly without notice, Walter Kihn turned toward Laura Dobbs and grabbed her gun barrel. Laura snarled and pulled the trigger. Walter Kihn fell. Shot in the chest. Walter's motion to snatch the barrel sent the gun flying across the ballroom floor. The officer waiting in the kitchenette doorway tackled Laura Dobbs from behind. She fell hard with a thud to the floor. She groaned.

"Call an ambulance!" Amanda shouted kneeling at her father's side. She pressed her hands into his chest trying to stop the bleeding. The blood was spurting from his body covering the ballroom floor in a red circle. The studio staff was just getting to work. They stared at the floor – a man lying on the floor with blood pooled around his torso, his daughter kneeling on the floor with tears streaming down her face, a woman in handcuffs with uniformed officers surrounding her, and Megan crawling out from behind the reception desk in an emerald green dress now wrinkled and crushed.

Sydney helped Megan stand up and smooth out her skirt. Carson demanded, "What is going on here?"

Megan gathered the staff in the back room when the ambulance had hauled Mr. Kihn to the hospital on a stretcher, and Laura Dobbs was led to the squad car.

Carson sat at his desk with KC perched on a stool next to him. Kelly Clark Johns was squeezed between Annalea Montgomery and Carl Young. Paddy and Stephanie held hands in the corner. Mary and Claire stood in the doorway as Chandler Dane arrived – Megan had called him as soon as Laura was apprehended. He wore a gray t-shirt and ragged jeans – certainly not studio attire. He leaned against the doorframe with his arm loosely draped over Claire's shoulder. She looked up at him with wide eyes and smiled.

Megan told the group about Laura's confession. How Mr. Kihn hired her to kill Edward Garrett. Then she told them about Ashley – that Mr. Kihn was her father. Everyone gasped. This part of the story was totally unexpected. They sat silently trying to digest the whole situation. Not all of them knew who Mr. Kihn and Amanda Garrett were. Nor did they connect the death of Edward Garrett to this studio. They seemed quite shocked by the entire story. There were whispers across the room. Chandler Dane however, smiled and nodded. The mystery was over. And he had been a part in solving it.

Later that day the news was updated. Mr. Kihn was in serious condition but would pull through. He had a police guard 24/7 however, because when he was ready to leave the hospital, he was expected to be charged with murder. His patient saintly wife initially stood by her husband's side but rumor had it she was considering divorce. Laura Dobbs or Laura Hamilton which proved to be her real name, was charged with murder and kidnapping. Ashley Dobbs was released. She was not present during the murder and although she obviously knew about the kidnapping, the police decided not to press charges. She had not been informed until the arrest of her mother that Amanda Kihn's father was her father as well. Who knew how she felt about this news.

The fall was beginning to show its colorful side. The wind became crisped and the apple orchards began to bring pickers for the sweet fruit. The oak and maple trees began to turn from a summery green to the yellows, oranges and reds of fall. Soon they would drop their leaves all together, and Minneapolis would expect a cold winter.

Megan scampered into the studio with the collar of her coat turned up to shield her neck and ears. For some reason today of all days she had forgotten a hat. When she reached the studio Carson was already in practicing his choreography for a future staff routine. Kelly Clark Johns was seated behind the reception desk charting her front department lessons for the week. Her efficiency was proving to be an asset.

When Megan entered, Kelly motioned to her. "Could we talk?"

Megan smiled but inside she frowned. Was she quitting, was she complaining or was she just plain whining? Whatever, it wasn't going to be good. Megan hung up her coat and prepared with a sigh for the problem of the day. What would it be today?

Kelly Clark Johns didn't drag it out. "I'm getting a divorce," she announced unemotionally. Megan nodded. Not a surprise. She had watched the sad state of high energy Kelly followed around by a beaten down James. It hadn't been a good match from the start.

But Kelly continued, "And I'm marrying Carl Young."

Megan reeled. This was unexpected. "And what about his wife, the lovely Annalea Montgomery?" she asked with eyebrow raised.

"Well, of course those two are getting a divorce as well. And James and Annalea are getting married to each other!" Kelly chirped hands spread palms out as if problem solved.

Megan sighed. "So now I suppose you will be known as Kelly Clark Johns Young."

At that Kelly laughed. "I suppose I should cut out a few of those names one of these days."

Megan wandered into Edward Garrett's office. The big cherry desk was still in the middle of the floor. His photos of Amanda and his primitive artwork were still there. No one had touched this office since his death. Megan stretched out in his comfy chair and pondered this last development. It began with Edward and Amanda — the string of relationships in this studio. That first relationship ended in divorce and death. Then came Jim Peterson and Annie St. Germaine. Those two were going strong. They had stopped into the studio just last week to

243

announce their pregnancy. It was nice to have one blessed moment come out of a marriage. Then there had been Carl and Annalea — short lived but on to new relationships. Of course Paddy and Stephanie were still planning their own wedding. It would be a big one. Then Kelly Clark Johns and James. That one was over too. But they would be switching partners and hopefully finding their soul mates. Carson and KC hadn't announced anything but friendship — thankfully. But it looked like Chandler and Claire were a new budding relationship as well. Mary and Sydney along with Megan were thankfully single. Megan pondered the past few months. She felt engulfed with relationships — drama and more relationships. It was stifling.

She made her way back to the reception area. Kelly was nowhere to be seen. She was probably back in the teachers' office or out for a quick cup of coffee. Not matter. Megan slid behind the desk and gazed at the schedule for the day. It was packed. She had to admit it was much busier since Kelly took over the new student department. They could accommodate more students and faster than previously. It was now possible to schedule people as soon as possible rather than waiting a few days for an opening. The front door bell rang. She looked up and met the gaze of a man. He was medium height with dark hair – thinning a bit around his temple. He smiled at her. She found herself not wanting to take her eyes from his face. His eyes seemed glued to her as well.

"May I help you?" she offered.

"I'd like information about dance lessons," he asked leaning on the top of the desk.

Megan began her spiel. She had it down perfectly. "When can I come in for a lesson?" he asked staring into her eyes. "As soon as possible. Today?" His head tilted to the side.

Megan knew without even looking down at the schedule there was nothing for today, but she also knew she had a few slots opened herself. She normally didn't teach lessons, but why not?

"Would you like to have lunch and come back for a lesson at 3:00? I'll teach you myself," she offered with a grin on her face.

"Perfect!" he replied and smiled back. "Just perfect!" He turned to leave but before opening the door looked back one more time at the woman behind the desk. His heart began to pound a bit faster. He smiled at her, and she smiled back. She had managed to stand and lean over the desk covering quite sufficiently the "No Student-Teacher Fraternization" sign with a large notebook. No need for him to read it! Not yet.

Epilogue: One Year Later

Despite Edward Garrett's death, the dance studio under the parking ramp remained strong with the new leadership. Walter Kihn recovered nicely and was promptly charged with murder along with Laura Dobbs. Both were convicted and sentenced to lengthy prison terms. The saintly Mrs. Kihn divorced her husband and has since found a new relationship with a man with little money but a huge heart and an honest character. She is extremely happy.

Amanda Garrett remains in contact with her new half sister Ashley Dobbs who returned to New Orleans and the studio there after her mother's conviction. Things in Ashley's life seemed strangely settled and normal after the departure of her overbearing parent. Her dancing has impressively developed. She has found a new dance partner – purely platonic this time – and is becoming a nationally known name in the ballroom dance arena. Amanda has remained single and unattached. Happily so it seems.

Annie and Jim Peterson had a baby and word has it are expecting another one. Kelly Clark Johns Young and Carl did indeed marry. They are extremely monogamous – probably for the first time in either of their young lives. They are still at the studio teaching and counseling but have also announced they are expecting and are looking to buy a large house in a distant suburb that seems more rural than urban. Their upcoming departure would not be unexpected news.

Annalea quit her job at the studio and announced her engagement to James. But they both seem quite content with a long, long engagement. Occasionally they stop in to update Megan with news of their travels and corporate jobs. Annalea now wears heels and suits rather than the character shoes she used to find flattering. Her makeup and hair look rather stylish and sophisticated – a tribute to Amanda's amazing instructions. Both Annalea and James seem to chatter a bit more... It seems they have much more to talk about and maybe someone else who actually listens.

Stephanie and Paddy are nearing their wedding date. Their year has been one of extreme planning. Stephanie has found great pleasure in finding just the right gown, flowers, cake, reception venue, band, etc. The event should be an amazing and successful day for both Stephanie and Paddy as well as the rest of the studio staff. Everyone has been deeply involved with plans bringing in bride magazines and music cuts for the pair to review, sampling cake and pouring over menus. It's been an interesting year for all and a new joint project for staff and students alike. Rumor has it they have an amazing Waltz routine choreographed for their first dance.

Carson and KC remain friends. That's all. Just friends. And Megan Meeker? She has also announced her engagement. Yes, that lone student who wandered in that fateful morning is indeed the groom to be. Then Megan Meeker will soon become the very generic Mrs. John Jones. Who would have guessed? In ten years would she be happy? A fortune teller would tell you a resounding "no". But who believes in fortune tellers?

WALTZ

The Waltz has two tempos — the slow Waltz and the faster Viennese Waltz. The timing for both is in ¾ time.

Waltz Basic Box Step:

Man's part — Forward with the left foot (count 1), Side right foot (2), Close left foot to right (3), Back with the right foot (1), Side left foot (2), Close right foot to left (3).

Lady's part — Back with the right foot (1), Side left foot (2), Close right foot to left (3), Forward with the left foot (count 1), Side right foot (2), Close left foot to right (3).

Lady's Underarm Turn Right:

Man's part — Dance two box steps leading lady to turn to her right (an outside turn) when stepping back on the second half of the first box. Lift the left arm to turn the lady and release the right hand on her back as she begins to turn under the arm regaining dance position when she finishes her turn.

Lady's part – ½ box, Forward (left foot) stepping into the man to begin a turn to the right under the man's lifted arm. Turn in a large circle with a total of 6 forward steps ending back with your partner and a side (right foot), close left to right. Regain dance position.

The faster Viennese Waltz requires special movements and patterns. The basic pattern is the **Hesitation:**
Man's part – Forward left foot (1 — hold 2, 3), Back right foot (1 — hold 2, 3), Side left (1 — hold 2, 3), Side right (1 — hold 2, 3).
Lady's part – Back right foot (1 — hold 2, 3), Forward left foot (1 — hold 2, 3), Side right (1 — hold 2, 3), Side left (1 — hold 2, 3).

Hesitation with Lady's Underarm Turn Right:
Man's part — Repeat all the foot patterns for the Man's Hesitation but release the lady and push away on the back hesitation and turn the lady to her right (outside turn) on the movement to the left side regaining dance position on the side right movement.
Lady's part – Back right foot (1, 2, 3), Back left foot retaining right hand hold with man (1, 2, 3), Side right beginning to turn right (1) step forward with left foot pushing to turn (2) and replace weight to stationary right foot (3), Side left regaining dance position.

www.ingramcontent.com/pod-product-compliance
Lightning Source LLC
Chambersburg PA
CBHW071144170626
46809CB00002B/755